Other Books by Trilogy Davis

Odessa and the First Constellation

When Life Gives You Pineapples

The Legends of Damasyr Book 3 Coming Soon!

Arabella

AND THE
TOWER OF MAGIC

Trilogy Davis

Trilogy Effect, LLC

This is a work of fiction. Names, characters, places, and incidents either are the product of the author's imagination or are used fictitiously. Any resemblance to actual persons, living or dead, events, or locales is entirely coincidental.

First paperback edition December 2023

ISBN 979-8-9867960-5-5 (paperback)

www.trilogyeffect.net

Dedicate this to my brothers man I'm moving like Itachi

Happy Birthday Isaiah!

ROYAL FOREST
JEMNY
ROYAL LAKE
JEMNAN AID TOWER
RUTABAGA AID TOWER
BJORN
LAKE ZAEBOS
ZAEBOS
NORTH T
RUTABAGA MOUNTAINS
LAKE ELYSE
TERZA A TOWER
ROZABAGA RIVER
ELYSE RIVER
ELYSE CREEK
ALMONASTIAN AID TOWER
NORTH DRESDEN
LAKE VICTORIA
DRESDENIAN AID TOWER
SOUTH DRESDEN
ALMONASTER
LAKE TAMBER
THE WETLANDS
FALLING STAR CRATER
DRIEN AID TOWER
STARSHINE
DR
LAKE LEDONIA
ICHORIAN AID TOWER
STARSHINE MOUNTAINS
ADDEMIRE PLATEAU
ICHOR
TAWNI MIRAGE
FORT ROSHNI
NORI DESERT
JACKDAW MOUNTAINS

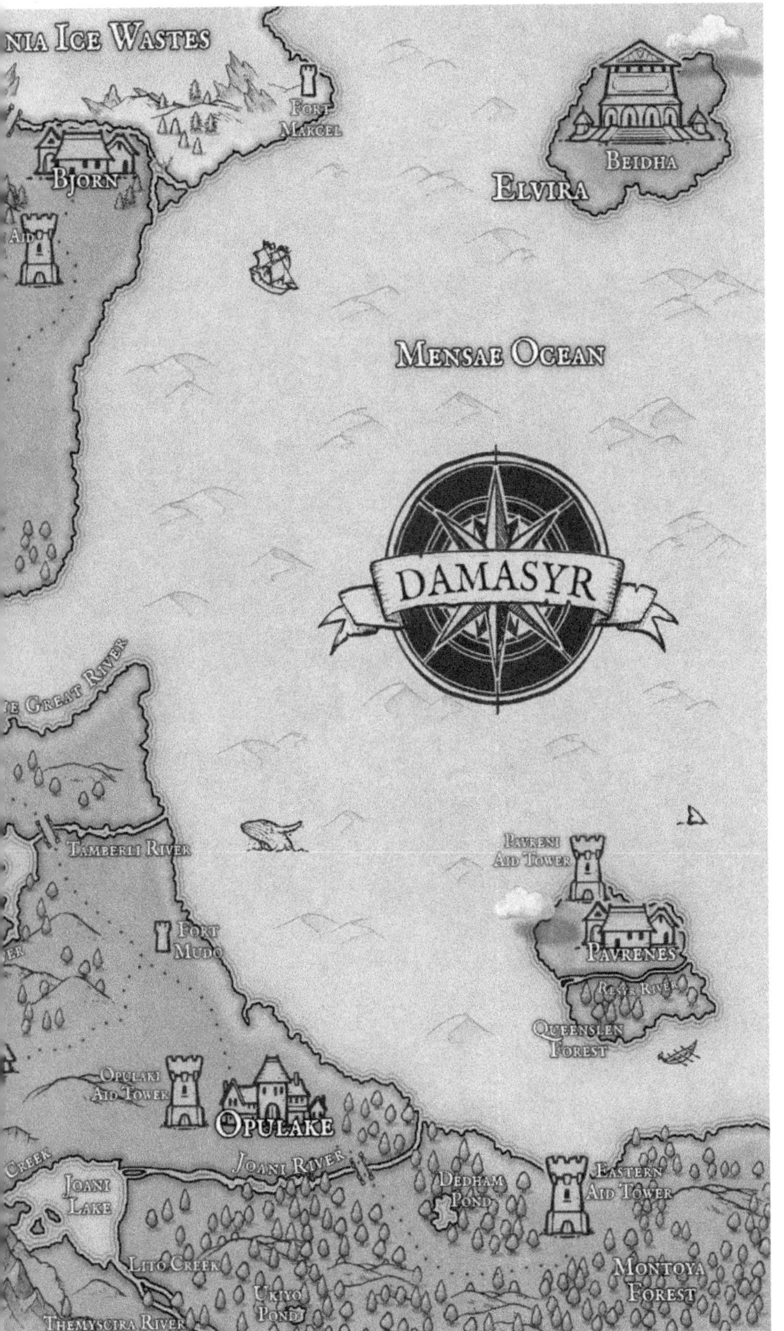
NIA ICE WASTES
FORT MARCEL
BJORN
AID
ELVIRA
BEIDHA
MENSAE OCEAN
DAMASYR
E GREAT RIVER
TAMBERLI RIVER
FORT MUDO
PAVRENI AID TOWER
PAVRENES
RESTE RIVER
QUEENSLEN FOREST
OPULAKI AID TOWER
OPULAKE
JOANI RIVER
DEDHAM POND
EASTERN AID TOWER
CREEK
JOANI LAKE
LITO CREEK
UKIYO POND
MONTOYA FOREST
THEMYSCIRA RIVER

Table of Contents

Chapter ONE *opulake* 1

Chapter TWO *samson* 15

Chapter THREE *olympia* 34

Chapter FOUR *freya* 47

Chapter FIVE *gorin* 62

Chapter SIX *hua* 75

Chapter SEVEN *frey* 90

Chapter EIGHT *savant* 101

Chapter NINE *mystio* 115

Chapter TEN *eloah* 126

Chapter ELEVEN *eufaula* 143

Chapter TWELVE *arabella* 154

Chapter THIRTEEN *hong tao* 166

Chapter FOURTEEN *imperi* 181

Chapter FIFTEEN *odessa* 192

Chapter SIXTEEN *micah* 204

Chapter SEVENTEEN *oqubay* 222

Chapter EIGHTEEN *ambrocio* 234

Chapter NINETEEN *estella*......................................249

Chapter TWENTY *tinosa* 259

Chapter TWENTY-ONE *shovi*......................................270

The World of Alphan II 283

Glossary 289

About The Author 298

Chapter ONE

opulake

It was a peculiar thing being the last of your kind.

I, of course, was not the last human in all of Damasyr, but after the sacking of my hometown, Opulake, by the mercenary group called the First Constellation I was the last surviving member of the town.

I was the last Opulaki.

I closed my eyes and sat on my former bed. When I had last slept in it my life was completely different. I was still adapting to my new reality, but without the framework of my upbringing in the Church of Eloah, I felt lost.

After my encounter with Odessa of Pavrenes, we had teamed up together and defeated a leader in the First

Constellation named Samson. After his defeat we were able to save her younger sister, Talicia, and we had gained our freedom.

I was not sure what freedom meant anymore though. I could go anywhere in Damasyr, but it would be an aimless journey.

I had been raised most of my adult life by an Elohan leader named, Tripa Fons in the settlement of Opulake. He had raised me and another girl named Estella.

We had been placed into the service of Eloah after our parents had sailed east to a country called Tyvent on a missionary trip.

The purpose of their journey was not purely for conversion but also to find a magical item called an *imperi*.

Our parents had also gone with some other Opulakis and although they were only supposed to be gone a little over one year they had yet to return.

I had been fourteen when the party had departed, and I was eighteen now. It had been four years since I had last seen them. Neither my parents, nor Estella's parents, or any other Opulaki from the mission, had returned to Opulake.

Tripa Fons was a hard man and took the commands of Eloah very seriously. He raised Estella and I within the commandments and when we failed to reach his standard we were punished and often whipped.

Despite this his death had greatly affected me. The thought of him missing felt like being stranded in the ocean with no boat or raft and it was only a matter of time before I went under.

Losing Tripa Fons felt like losing my father twice and Samson's words about his death circled through my mind.

He died quickly and on his knees.

A holy man crying out for his pathetic god.

On top of the loss of Tripa Fons I had also been betrothed to an Opulaki man named Skylark. He was strong and lean but despite this he had been killed by Samson on day six of the occupation.

I had not been close to Skylark; he was more focused on fishing than on the words of Eloah. Besides that, he was a notorious flirt with the other women of Opulake, but Tripa Fons had negotiated the marriage on my behalf with Skylark's parents.

Skylark was by no means ugly, but his wit had not gone further than his abs. His family had a last name in their family and Skylark was only one great deed from the Queen restoring it and his last name would in turn become mine.

I cared little of last names, but I figured I could have done worse. I had no dowry to bring into the marriage and that limited my options.

But now Skylark was dead.

Tripa Fons was dead.

Estella was dead.

My town was in shambles and my parents may never return. Even if they did, the state of Opulake was hardly a fitting welcome for someone who had devoted years of their lives to the church.

So, after Samson had been defeated, I had been left like a koi in a pond. There was no one to tell me where I could go or what I could do next.

There was no one to tell me where I *should* go or what I *should* do next. I was left to pray on it and hope for a feeling or sign from Eloah guiding me towards whatever destination he had for me.

I had considered following my new friend, Odessa, to her home in Pavrenes, but there was nothing there for me. It was her home and community. She belonged there and I did not.

I had also thought about finding a ship to Tyvent to search for my parents but ships to the far east were rare and very expensive and I had little money. I had not given up on the idea, but it was not something I could easily accomplish.

Instead of going with Odessa I had decided to stick with the Mystio, Savant Solace and Micah Zhang, who had come to Opulake to end the First Constellation occupation.

Mystio were soldiers who were specially trained in Jemny, the capital city of Damasyr. Opulake had previously had two other Mystio stationed here. One was named Eufaula O'Connor and the other was named Velma.

Both had been killed by Samson on the first day of occupation after the Battle of Three Sides.

I knew wherever the Mystio went I would not be bored. They were journeying to Fort Mudo to deliver the murderer Samson, and I looked forward to the deliverance of justice on the behalf of all the dead Opulakis.

We would be in Fort Mudo for some time as we waited for the other Mystio named Adonis. Adonis had volunteered to get Odessa to Pavrenes to meet us in Fort Mudo before the Mystio went to Jemny.

I had traveled to Drie and South Dresden before but had never been to Fort Mudo. The military forts of Damasyr were restricted to only those with special clearances.

Even when we traveled for church business, we had never been permitted to enter the Fort, so we had never traveled northeast.

Adonis had gone with Odessa and her younger sister, Talicia, to Pavrenes to make sure the people there received the plagicine for the plague that had been ravaging the kingdom.

I thought of the futility in rebelling against Lord Laurens for more plague tonics just to be captured and murdered by the First Constellation after we had weakened ourselves in a civil war.

I had been blessed by Eloah to have been the last survivor. If I had not been left because I was fat, I would have been dead in the place of another Opulaki. At the thought I gave another prayer of thanks to Eloah for his mercy.

"Are you good to go, Arabella?"

Savant's voice broke me out of my thoughts.

I looked up and saw Savant looking at me, concern gleaming in his black eyes.

I tightened the strings on my bag and threw it on my back. I flashed Savant a modest smile and nodded my head.

He had insisted on coming with me to my room in the Opulaki Church of Eloah, even though I knew it was difficult for him to be here.

The congregation hall above us had been transfigured into a makeshift arena and it was there that his *inamorata* Eufaula had been killed. She was one of the Mystio here and her death greatly affected Savant.

An *inamorata* was a spiritual bond of love reserved for the deepest loves and when committed, the partners became completely empathetic of each other.

It was safe to say that it was not a bond I expected to get with Skylark, Eloah bless him.

I walked to the doorway of my room and glanced back at the room once more. I pictured Estella, I, and Tripa Fons praying together every Friday night when our moon, Ithil, was at its perigee.

Arabella and the Tower of Magic

I sighed and walked through the hallway and into Estella's room. I strode over to a loose stone in the wall and removed it.

In the hidden cache was a pouch with gold coins that Estella kept hidden there. With her death she would not need them anymore, so I took the pouch and placed it in my pocket.

We had both been planning on sailing east to Tyvent to search for our parents but without Estella the idea of that quest seemed insurmountable.

It was hard to believe the white and black-haired girl was dead. I had seen her get stabbed by one of the bandits during the Battle of Three Sides and she had never been jailed with the other Opulakis during the occupation.

She had been so strong and was an expert Morale. But many other strong Opulakis had fallen to the brute force of the bandits.

I knelt into her bedside nightstand and retrieved her journal and the jewelry her parents had left her. The metal and gems had been Estella's highest possessions and now I would guard them for her.

Together Savant and I climbed the stairs of the temple and trudged through the sandy makeshift arena in the congregation area of the church. The blood that stained the sand was sacrilege as the use of weapons and the act of bloodshed in the church was *vetiti,* which meant it was forbidden.

The sand would have to be removed and the temple would need to be reblessed after all the death that had taken place there, but it was only a matter of time before the Elohans would do so, even if the town itself remained in ruins.

The location of the temple had been chosen by the First Prophet Rutabaga Zaebos himself after he received the vision from Eloah that showed him a map of the kingdom with six locations marked on it.

Those six locations would grow to be Opulake, Ichor, Jemny, Zaebos, and Dresden would have two although eventually it was split into South Dresden and North Dresden fulfilling Rutabaga's vision of six temples in six settlements dedicated to Eloah.

So, it was only a matter of time before a new Tripa or the prophet herself would make their way down to Opulake to reestablish the temple. If the Mystio knew of the attack by the First Constellation already then, the Church of Eloah would not be long behind them.

The closest temple to the one in Opulake was to the north in South Dresden and it was farther north than Fort Mudo where Savant and his squad were heading to.

We would have to pass through South Dresden on the way to Jemny and it was there I figured my path with the Mystio would diverge. They would go on to Jemny and I would rejoin the church there in South Dresden until I had reestablished my place in the world.

Despite them rebuilding the temple no one could return the Eternal Flame. The Eternal Flame appeared a normal bonfire, yet its flames were green and had been burning for a thousand years before the First Constellation had quenched it.

It was a shame as I did not have the knowledge of how the First Prophet had lit the flame. The information had been lost when Dresden was flooded and split into two cities.

I followed Savant out of the temple into the light of our elder star Zaniah which was already shining on us. It was the morning after Odessa had departed and after a horrible night of rest we were preparing to depart for Fort Mudo.

I wrinkled my nose in disgust. The air still smelled like burning flesh and death.

In front of the Opulaki Aid Tower the other Mystio, whose name was Micah, tended to the horses and made sure that our supplies were attached properly.

Micah and Savant had only two remaining horses, as the extra horse they had brought had been given to Odessa and Talicia. Odessa had needed the horse because her mission was a race against time and the sooner they could deliver the plagicine to the Pavrenes the more Pavrenis they could save.

I coughed and hoped I was not getting sick. The Mystio had given me the plagicine and we hoped it would work against the plague even though I had not shown any symptoms. There was a chance that it only worked on those who were already sick with the plague and there was no way to prevent it.

The horses were Mystio horses and were specially bred for the work the Mystio did. The Mystio could signal to them with certain hand signs and whistles. Both horses had been attached to a cart which was to hold the bandit lieutenant Samson.

Savant's horse was named Chalk Snout. It was a funny name, but Savant had told me he had named the horse when he was much younger and Mystio horses were never renamed.

Chalk Snout had golden tan fur with a ghostly white mane. At the top of Chalk Snout's muzzle was a line of white as if someone had used chalk and drawn down from the top of his head down to his nose.

Micah's horse was named Tachyon. Tachyon was larger than Chalk Snout and according to Micah was the fastest horse in all of Damasyr. He had a shiny black coat that seemed to shimmer even at night.

I glanced at the Opulaki Aid Tower which reached towards the sky. It was one of the oldest buildings in Opulake and was designed by the First Prophet himself, but it had not escaped the carnage of the First Constellation.

The large wooden door had been blown off and the rock foundation was damaged in several places. Despite this it could still serve its initial purpose of being an emergency beacon as at the top there was a large brazier that when lit could be seen by the other nearby aid towers.

During the attack by the First Constellation the lord of Opulake, Lord Laurens, had been barricaded in the tower as he had converted it into a living space, and we had been caught off guard by the bandits and the tower was never lit.

I had asked Savant if we should light the tower now, but he had said that there was no point. Lighting the aid tower would draw in those from the other nearby aid towers but there would be no one left in Opulake to assist leaving their own settlements exposed.

His logic made sense but I longed for the church to come to Opulake and rebuild the church here. Despite this I deferred to him for the decision and had not complained when he'd answered.

"Good morrow," I said to Micah with a smile.

They looked up and saw Savant and I approaching. They snapped to a stiff position of attention and saluted Savant.

"Relax, Micah," Savant said after returning the salute. "Are we ready to depart yet?"

Micah nodded their head and then smiled back at me.

Micah was rarely seen without a smile and the smile always brightened their golden-brown eyes. Their eyes were slanted, and they had short black hair with a bald fade on the side.

"Just got to stake the flag and put Samson in here," they said with a smile.

They reached into a sack on Chalk Snout and pulled out a flag split into three pieces. Micah quickly assembled it and handed it to me.

"Want to do the honors?" Micah asked. "After all this is your home."

I gripped the flag with both of my hands tightly and nodded. I strode over to the Church of Eloah and with a grunt slammed the flag into the ground in front of it.

It went several inches into the ground and after a second shove it was successfully planted into the ground. It stood about six feet tall, and the wind caught the flag revealing a white swan on a purple background.

White and purple were the Damasyri standard, and the white swan was the symbol of the Mystio.

I was not sure if the flag would actually do anything. Everything valuable in Opulake had been stolen already and all its people were already dead. Even all the horses were gone.

Despite this, placing the flag did make me feel better. I had faith that the city would be restored once the temple was restored.

Now was the hard part. We had to successfully contain the giant of a man that was Samson in the metal cart so that he could be escorted to Fort Mudo with us.

The cart had limited space and could normally fit four or five people but with Samson, Savant did not want to take any chances.

He chose to put Samson alone in the cart and the other bandits we had captured were left in cages until more soldiers could arrive to escort them too.

The previous night Savant had sent pigeons to the Mystio in Drie and Fort Mudo requesting soldiers to transport the bandits but, in the meantime, they had been left with as much food and water as we could spare.

I felt bad for them, yet it was not long ago that the tables had been turned and it was I who had been caged and I remembered the bandits who had sneered and spit at me.

I focused on my Faith and my neon green aura appeared.

"Do you need help with Samson?" I asked nervously.

Despite days of rest and magical healing my stomach still felt sore and churned at the thought of facing Samson again. If it had not been for Odessa, I would have died along with everyone else in Opulake.

Micah smiled and shook their head.

"He's strong alright, but he's no match for me," they said.

"That may be true, but I'll also be assisting just in case," Savant said.

It was hard to believe that Micah alone was strong enough to fight Samson. So many had died against him, even other Mystio such as Eufaula and Velma.

It had been a great ordeal for Odessa and I to even damage him let alone defeat him. There was no way Micah alone could beat him as easily as they projected.

I nodded my head and looked at the Mystio building where Samson was being contained. My breathing shuddered with anticipation.

Savant studied the flag to make sure it was planted securely and then he gestured to Micah and together they entered the building containing the bandits of the First Constellation.

Despite their words I said a prayer to Eloah and manifested my Faith. It flickered uncertainly and I rubbed my fingers together.

After a moment Micah emerged from the building and ran towards Tachyon and Chalk Snout. Savant quickly followed him and gestured for me to follow him quickly.

I ran as fast as I could, which was not very fast, and met them at the cart. Savant grabbed the ropes and Micah reached out their hand and helped me climb into the front seat of the cart.

"What's going on?" I asked looking from Savant to Micah. "Where's Samson?"

The horses bolted down the road towards the gate of the town and I fell onto Micah who caught me and helped me sit up.

"Samson is gone," Micah said.

Chapter TWO

samson

My heart dropped into a pitch-black chasm.

How could Samson have escaped?

Where could he be going?

Was he coming after me for revenge, or was he after Odessa instead?

"Where do you think he is?" I asked the Mystio, and Micah shrugged as they pulled out their throwing knives and began to carefully sharpen them.

"It's hard to say," Savant admitted. "He could be scampering back to their leader, Jesuit, and the rest of the First Constellation, or he could be going after Odessa for revenge. You might know the most about him personally, Arabella. What do you think? We will have to gamble on his route and hope we guess correctly. Micah, I would like to hear your thoughts also."

I was surprised he was asking us. The leaders in the Church of Eloah never asked for suggestions or feedback; they simply did what they wanted and everyone else did what they were told. I was silent thinking about this so Micah spoke first.

"Well, Odessa has Adonis with her, and I have no doubt he could take Samson down solo. On top of that Odessa was strong enough to help Arabella beat Samson and can also Channel. Between the two of them I think they will be fine. Arabella even showed Talicia Channeling basics. That said, Samson may not know Odessa is protected by Adonis."

I looked at Micah as they spoke, hanging on to their every word. Their face was serious for once as they shared their thoughts.

"I think Samson had his pride broken and from what we know of Jesuit he won't take Samson back after such a defeat. I think he'll be out for revenge or redemption and that we should follow after Odessa towards Pavrenes."

Savant nodded his head and then glanced at me awaiting my thoughts. I cleared my throat before speaking and when I did speak my voice cracked and I groaned internally.

"I do not think Samson will go after Odessa," I said finally after thinking hard. "His pride is wounded yes, but he knows you Mystio will be on his tail, so the question is does he think he can find Odessa before we can find him? I think he will probably go back to the First Constellation to recover first, even if he will be punished for his failure."

I finished speaking, conscious that my analysis was much shorter than Micah's and awaited Savant's decision.

Savant nodded his head again as I finished. The cart hit a nasty bump and shook violently. The force of the bump caused me to lean onto Micah's shoulder.

I blushed and apologized, but Micah only smiled at me and helped me readjust myself. We continued to speed down the road and it was quiet as Savant took a moment to think before he spoke.

"Let's head to the ocean," Savant decreed. "We haven't been able to find their base and based off of where they sunk the *Estonia* I'm thinking they're somewhere near the shore or in a boat."

His reasoning made sense to me, and even though he had taken my side I was not super excited to be facing Samson again even with the strength of Micah and Savant on my side.

I could feel the pain already coming from the fight and my stomach began to throb where Samson had kneed me in the gut.

I placed my hand on my stomach hoping to ease the discomfort and started to regret my decision to not go with Odessa to Pavrenes. The thought of facing the murderer of my town made me sweat.

I considered asking to be let off. I could travel to Drie, the closest settlement to Opulake. It was in the north and without a horse it would take several days to arrive there, but I would be going the opposite direction of where we thought Samson would be.

No.

I was scared but I was not a coward. Samson deserved justice for what he had done. He could not be allowed to roam and cause further destruction.

Opulake was not far from the coast and we could reach it in a day with good travel conditions. The skies were clear over us but in the distance, I could see a storm brewing to the south.

It was a cold day, and the wind tore at my face angrily. Tears of fear began to form at the edges of my eyes and when I blamed the wind it seemed that wind only increased its ferocity.

I was forced to periodically lower my eyelids to shield my eyes from the wind. The sky was dark, and I could see a large storm in the distance and the scent of rain was heavy in the air.

I was no fan of horseback riding; it was uncomfortable, and the constant bouncing made me feel lightheaded. That was under ideal conditions and the storm only made me feel more anxious.

It was not so bad riding in the cart at first but once we left the road towards the Mensae Ocean our travel conditions deteriorated.

Arabella and the Tower of Magic

We were silent as we rode, and it was quiet besides the constant clopping of Tachyon and Chalk Snout.

Zaniah soon made its descent, and we were left only with the light of the younger sun Astria. It would soon be night and we would be making camp soon.

The Mensae Ocean came into view, and I saw how vast it was. I did not see the ocean often but every time I did it struck me with wonder.

The Mensae Ocean seemed to be endless, yet I knew it did have an end, and that my parents were in Tyvent, a land across the sea.

I remember begging them not to leave but my father had only kissed me on the cheek and boarded *Green Flame* without looking back. He had wiped his face with his sleeve and told my mother to join him.

My mother had gripped my hand lightly and pulled me tightly into a hug. I felt her tears hitting the top of my head and remembered how I had overheard her telling my father that she did not wish to go.

My father had volunteered and if his mission was successful, he would be promoted to the rank of Tripa, and we would be sent to South Dresden to manage the Church of Eloah there.

But he never returned, and the post was given to someone else, and I was left in the care of Tripa Fons with Estella.

I thought of what Samson might be up to. He had been knocked unconscious by Odessa, but he had received no permanent damage.

I shuddered at the thought of Jesuit, the leader of the First Constellation. It was crazy that someone could be stronger than that monster.

"Do you know who the other lieutenant is of the First Constellation?" I asked the Mystio.

Savant shook his head.

"We know of the leader, Jesuit, the lieutenant Samson and the lieutenant captain Olympia," Savant replied.

I hated the unknown. It was highly possible that we would have to fight all of the leaders of the First Constellation at once.

I had only one fight under my belt, and I had ended it unconscious. The win definitely was gained by Odessa, and I did not want to be dead weight in the next fight we had.

Odessa was an inspiration to me and I longed to be more like her. Usually, she exuded an aura of confidence but I knew she had a human side. When I had first met her, she had been crying in her cell.

I had seen in her memories through our empathy link how she and her younger sister Talicia had been trained since they were younger by her father. Odessa and Talicia had the training to keep up in a fight.

I smiled at the thought of Talicia. She had deep blue eyes and flaming red hair. She was a young girl, only twelve years old, yet she had been through a lot with Odessa to get the cure for their father.

While Odessa had recovered from our fight with Samson I had taught Talicia the basics of Elohan Faith Magic. Odessa had woken up and immediately returned to her mission. She was so relentless.

I considered contacting her magically and letting her know that Samson had escaped but I decided otherwise, considering getting home to her father with the plagicine would be her number one priority. I did not want to distract her if it wasn't necessary.

Odessa was a hurricane, blowing away any obstacles to protect her family. She refused to ever give up regardless of the obstacles. She had an entire family and town to protect, and I had nothing left to protect; that was the big difference between us.

I wanted to be more like Odessa. I wished she was here with us now or that I could feel her mind, but I could not. Her mind felt like a strong breeze blowing through my head, but I hadn't felt it since she had left Opulake with Adonis.

An empathy link was a spiritual link between two or more people. I had created it to save Odessa's life after our fight with Samson and now we could speak to each other mentally and give each other energy.

The only downside was that our lives were also linked. If either of us died the other would die too so I made sure to be extra careful.

My fists gripped the fabric of my green dress and I exhaled slowly. I tried to think of other types of magic I could maybe learn to increase my combat effectiveness. I could use my Faith relatively well compared to the other Opulakis, but I had trouble using it offensively.

I knew of Mages who used Elemental Magic. They could control fire and water, but I had no idea how to learn it or who could teach me.

There were also Djinni who made bargains with spirits. Warlocks were similar as they bartered with other nonplanar entities for power. The idea of bargaining with an otherworldly force also seemed like a bad idea.

True the humans received great power but at any moment their deity could take away their power on a whim or if the human disobeyed or did something their deity did not approve of.

I knew the Mystio could do something called Channeling, which was similar to Elohan Faith Magic, perhaps they could help me train my magic.

Faith, feelings, intent.

To get stronger I had to increase my Faith, but how did I do that? There were no Elohans here to guide me. Once again, I concluded that I was on my own.

Perhaps there was a weapon I could train with, but I had never had any proficiency with a sword or spear or any other weapon. There had never been a reason to fight like that in Opulake.

Micah had a short sword and three throwing knives in a band on each forearm. Savant on the other hand wielded twin straight blade swords called chokuto.

I wondered if I could ask them to train me on the way to Fort Mudo after we had detained Samson. I had not yet brought it up because I did not want to be a bother.

I asked when we planned on stopping and Savant replied that we were not. I was surprised and we were going off of only the light of our moon, Ithil.

Ithil was partially blocked out by black clouds making it hard to see and as he spoke it began to rain lightly, obscuring our view even further.

"We can't afford to let Samson get away," Savant said. "If he gets to a boat or ship we'll have lost him; we don't have a boat to pursue him with and although there are methods used to walk on water none of them are fast enough to keep up with a boat for long."

His reasoning made sense and I yawned. Micah said something in my ear, but at the same time thunder roared and they were forced to repeat themselves.

"Tired already?" Micah repeated and I nodded.

I had slept better since being released from my cell, but I still had not had a good night of sleep to fully replenish my body.

I took my glasses off, cleaned the lenses with a clean part of my shirt and when I placed them back on my face, I could see something in the distance.

"Do you all see that?" I said pointing at the shape in the distance at the edge of the beach.

"Yes, I do," Savant said, and he urged Chalk Snout and Tachyon faster but it seemed both mounts were reaching their limit. They both whinnied in protest but despite this they did increase their pace slightly.

As we got closer, I recognized the running figure as Samson. He wore no shoes, and his legs were coated in mud and filth. His loincloth was drenched from the rain and it hung low on his waist.

"It is him!" I called out and Micah grinned.

"We got him," they said, and I had to agree.

There was nowhere else for Samson to flee to. He was trapped between us and the ocean. The horizon was clear of any boats or ships so there was nowhere for him to swim to.

Despite this he continued onwards towards the water, and I had to wonder if he could see something that we could not.

Chalk Snout and Tachyon neared closer, and Micah removed one of their throwing knives and readied it.

"Give the request," Savant grunted.

"Samson, halt, under the authority of Queen Hana!" Micah called.

Of course, Samson ignored us and after a nod from Savant, Micah aimed a throwing knife and sent it flying.

It cut through the air and landed in Samson's upper shoulder. I was impressed with Micah's aim. The rain had increased into a torrent and the wind was heavy and I heard Samson grunt in pain as he pulled the blade out and threw it down and into the sand.

Just as Samson reached the shore a large metal vehicle made out of black metal breached the surface of the water.

I had never seen anything like it. It was different from the wooden boats I had seen and had a metallic gleam to it. On the side of the metal boat in red writing was the name *Tinosa.* A square hatch clicked and swung open and out of it emerged a large woman.

The woman had grey eyes that seemed to glow through the storm at us and long black hair that clung to her back. Behind her another person emerged from the water machine.

It was a man with thin brown eyes and very low black hair. He, along with the woman, emerged and swam briefly onto the beach.

The woman was tall and although she was not as tall as Samson she towered over everyone else. The man who accompanied her was short, maybe only five foot four, yet next to the cowering Samson he looked all the more intimidating.

They wore the all black and red constellation symbol on their chests of the uniform of the First Constellation, and I tensed as we approached.

As Samson approached the woman she slapped him hard, and he froze. It was such a shock as I could not imagine anyone treating the powerful force that was Samson like that.

It scared me.

"You idiot," she snapped. "What are you doing here? Didn't I tell you to bring them south?"

Samson mumbled something that I could not hear, and Savant commanded Tachyon and Chalk Snout to halt.

He and Micah jumped from the cart and ran after Samson. I stumbled down and rushed after them towards the enemies.

"Turn around and fight," the man with black hair said.

Samson nodded and he slowly faced us.

Micah and Savant began to Channel as Samson charged us. Micah conjured an aura wall between us and Savant Channeled a wall behind our opponents so they could not return to the water vehicle.

Samson raised his fist and slammed it into the wall Micah had manifested and it shattered. It broke into shards like broken glass and faded away.

I was unsure how to contribute. It was three versus three and I knew each of our foes were as strong or stronger than Samson.

To my surprise the woman and the man did not intervene. They simply watched as Samson made his approach.

Samson charged towards Micah, probably because they were the smallest and the closest. Micah coated their arms with their aura and planted their feet.

When Samson was close to them Micah leaned forward and slipped between his legs. They stood quickly and chopped Samson quickly four times in the back with the edge of their cloaked hand.

Samson roared and just like that he fell into the sand unconscious. I was in shock that Micah had dealt with Samson so easily even if Samson was weakened.

Micah had not been simply boasting before and my jaw dropped as I looked at them. Micah shrugged like it was nothing and smiled at me.

"Micah!" Savant shouted.

Micah's smile faded and they turned swiftly to face the other bandits, but they were not fast enough. The First Constellation man balled his fist and plunged it into Micah's abdomen just under their chest piece.

Micah grunted in pain and licked their lips. They lifted their arms and began to Channel into them, but the man deftly pulled a pair of yellow bangles and latched one onto each of Micah's wrists.

As they clicked shut Micah's aura vanished and Micah threw up suddenly in the sand of the beach. The man grabbed Micah by the strap of their chest piece but before he could do more Savant appeared at Micah's side.

Savant coated his hand in his bordeaux aura and chopped it at the man's wrist. The man let go of Micah's armor and as Micah began to fall Savant reached for them to prevent them from falling to the ground.

Before Savant could catch Micah, the man swung another cuff towards Savant's wrist and Savant was forced to let Micah's body fall to the ground.

I rushed forward as they exchanged blows, and I grabbed Micah by their boots. I grunted from the effort and pulled them out of the immediate danger where the two men were fighting.

I glanced at the woman, but she only watched us with a small smile. She stood there with her arms crossed, her eyes still seeming to glow in the rain and gave me chills. She had not been involved in any other fighting and had not come forward to help Samson after his defeat, leaving him face down on the beach.

I heard Savant grunt and looked over as one of Savant's wrists was cuffed and his aura faded from that arm.

It did not seem like the First Constellation man was using any type of magic that I could see but he was extremely fast and for a while the two men had seemed even, but now Savant was lagging slightly.

Savant suddenly jumped back and with his right hand he produced a dagger made of bordeaux aura. He quickly threw it at the man's face.

The man moved quickly to close the distance between them and was not able to completely dodge the blade and it cut deeply into his face just below his right eye.

Blood dripped heavily down his face but by not dodging the blade the man was able to effectively cuff Savant's other wrist causing his magic to fade.

Savant's cheeks bulged as if he were going to throw up too, but he swallowed hard and swung his fist at the man.

Savant's blow was easily parried by the man who used his other hand to pull Savant by his chest armor and wrapped his fingers around Savant's throat.

He began to squeeze, and Savant pulled sideways, raised his arms, and slammed them into the man's arms twice breaking his grip.

I realized I had been paralyzed, simply watching the fight. I had to help.

Savant coughed and I ran forward and stood behind the man. I manifested my Faith into a wall as I'd seen Odessa do in the Opulaki Church of Eloah.

Instead of waiting for the man to break it I pushed the neon green construct into the man's back and forced him forward towards Savant.

Savant flexed his arms and managed to ram them into the man's neck in a lariat that finally brought the man to the ground.

I glanced down just in time to see the man grab me by the ankle. He gripped it hard, and I yelped as he pulled me forcefully. I lost my balance and fell and hit something hard on my head.

I looked up and saw a night sky full of stars. I struggled to focus and saw Savant still sparring with the bandit.

I was suddenly pulled onto my feet by the neck of my dress. The collar dug into my throat, and I coughed at the discomfort as I was dragged onto my feet.

"Olympia, you said you would not interfere," the man said without halting his sparring with Savant or looking away.

"I think we've wasted enough time, stop playing with the Mystio and let's go," Olympia said.

The man grunted and in a flash, he grabbed Savant by the back of his head and slammed his own head against Savant's forehead.

He released Savant and Savant stumbled backwards. He struggled to regain his balance, but it was apparent that the fight was over.

Savant continued to fight but he was much slower. The First Constellation man lazily deflected a few blows from Savant before he took two fingers and stabbed at a point in Savant's neck.

Savant gasped and without a word he fell into the sand next to Samson and didn't move anymore. Micah leaned forward and slowly stood up once more.

Olympia held me still as Micah stood up and faced the man. The man waited patiently as Micah struggled to remove some of their remaining throwing knives.

They exhaled deeply and then threw two knives at the man at once. Once they were in the air, they reached for their sword, but it was hard to reach with their hands cuffed.

Even though the man was only a couple of feet in front of Micah he managed to dodge the knives by turning sideways.

Micah managed to grip their sword and silently rushed the man. The man at the last moment parried them with a dagger with a red gem at the bottom of it that he seemed to pull out of nowhere.

There was a flash of sparks as the metal met and as the men parted the bandit leaned forward and low and brought his fist upwards slamming it into Micah's jaw.

Micah was lifted from the ground and landed on their back with their head slamming down hard on the front of Savant's Mystio chest plate.

It was up to me now it seemed, as I pulled hard against Olympia's grip, and she released me. I manifested my Faith and shaped it into a wall and slammed it into Olympia.

The maneuver seemed to catch her off guard and she fell into the sand on her butt. I was blessed to have surprised her, but I knew my blessings would be running out soon.

I turned to face the man, but he was in my face already. I saw the bandit man form two stiff fingers. He rushed me and shot out. His aim was for my neck and despite seeing it coming I was not fast enough to dodge it.

Instead, I exhaled quickly and manifested my Faith. It buzzed to life, and I willed it to wrap around my neck. The man's fingers bounced off my aura and I managed to stay standing a bit longer.

I had never used my Faith in such a manner and before Odessa I could not have imagined using it that way.

I glanced back at Olympia and saw her standing up and I took a step back so I could see both of them at once.

In contrast to Olympia's minor participation before now they both rushed me. I raised my hands to defend myself, but Olympia knocked them down easily with her own hands.

I rushed to lift them back up, but the force of Olympia's blows had forced them down to my side. I was not fast enough to bring my hands back up for protection and the man managed to move in and grip my neck firmly.

He began to squeeze, and I struggled and hit his hands and arms, but it was in vain. As I faded away, I wished desperately that Odessa was still here.

Chapter THREE

olympia

I dreamt of Eufaula O'Connor, one of the dead Mystio of Opulake.

The woman was three years older than me, but she was only twenty-one when she had died fighting Samson. I thought of Velma too. Both had been killed by Samson young with the potential for so many years snuffed.

He could not get away with it.

Eufaula sat at a desk constructing a letter for her boyfriend, Savant Solace. I had heard several stories about the mystery man she'd met while training in the capital, but Estella and I had never met him.

Estella had often teased that the pigeons simply flew off and pretended to deliver the letters and that there was no "Savant Solace".

While Velma and Eufaula had both been stationed in Opulake for a little over a year, Eufaula had actually lived in Opulake before enlisting.

Eufaula had initially lived in Drie, a settlement to the west but after the death of her parents she had moved to Opulake with her grandmother. She was dead now too thanks to the First Constellation.

We had been friends and her death loitered in my mind. I had finally met her Savant Solace, but Eufaula was gone, and I had hoped we could have all met together.

I had never been as close with Eufaula as I had been with Estella but when she was off duty and Tripa Fons did not require me, which was rare, we would stargaze and make up names for the stars and planets in the sky.

I knew I was dreaming. I manifested a body and then sat down in a newly generated patch of grass. I could not rush rest and would wake up when my body was ready.

We had lost the fight with the First Constellation. I could not believe it but because I was dreaming that meant I was still alive. I was unsure what the reason was but I was grateful to Eloah for his mercy; after all, if I died, so would Odessa because of our empathy link.

So, I was being held hostage, but why? What could they gain by keeping me alive? Perhaps I was to serve as bait for Odessa. They would let her know they had me and she would of course come for me, rushing into their trap.

I tried to reach out to her and warn her. I attempted to extend my mind, but my consciousness was restrained.

I had wondered if it was because I was unconscious or if the bandits had bound me in the magic suppressing cuffs I had seen them use on the Mystio.

I wondered if they had kept the Mystio alive also. I could not bear to lose them as well. We were not close, but Savant was the last attachment to Eufaula I had, and Micah had been nothing but kind to me since I had met them.

If they were dead, then the First Constellation would pay.

In fact, they would pay anyway.

I had been content following the Mystio where they went but I came to the conclusion that I should have been focused on avenging Opulake.

I knew I would have to train; I was fat and slow, and I could not use magic well enough.

I thought of Odessa and how resilient she was. She was a woman I aspired to be like, and she was still a year younger than me.

I sighed and crossed my legs and gripped my ankles. I arched my back and looked upwards. A sky and our suns, Astria and Zaniah appeared.

"Eloah, drive away all weakness from my body. Give me strength and know that I serve you and your people," I prayed.

After the prayer I rolled onto my stomach and leaned back onto my knees and palms. I knew that mental training could in turn make the body stronger. I had never needed to do so before, but desperate times called for desperate measures.

I did a push up.

o

My eyes burst open. I was awake and sweating heavily from my mental training. I exhaled deeply and groaned as a wave of fatigue hit me.

I leaned my head against the edge of something and looked around. Next to me were Micah and Savant.

I attempted to see if they were both alive, but I was unable to move. Two straps kept me pinned against the wall restricting my movements and my wrists were cuffed with the yellow stone bangles.

I stared until I saw both of their chests rise and let out a sigh of relief. They were both at the very least, alive.

Thank Eloah.

We were in a circular room of metal with windows that revealed dark blue water. It appeared we were in some sort of underwater boat, and I recalled how it had emerged from under the surface of the water when we had been on the beach.

At the front of the boat, I could see the man, Olympia, and Samson seated. Through the front glass I could see the murky water illuminated by a light of some sort.

Samson was conscious now and he leaned against a wall groaning in pain. He looked barbaric in nothing but a loincloth compared to the expensive clothes the others wore.

At the sight of him my anger simmered, and I gritted my teeth in response.

I thought of the great and pure souls that had been collected because of his violence. Why had they died, and he lived? Was it a question of strength or had they fallen out of the grace of Eloah?

I pulled against my restraints, but it was in vain. It seemed that my mental workout had not started to benefit me yet.

Samson heard me struggling and smiled at me. He stood and strode over to me and removed the straps that restrained me. Grabbing me by the neck he lifted me into the air and slammed my head into the metal ceiling.

I cried out in pain and felt the light wetness that came from the blood that leaked out of my scalp. A drop of the blood trailed down my forehead, in between my eyes, and curved around my lips.

"Samson," the man said evenly, and I felt Samson's grip loosen slightly. Samson hesitated for a moment then released me.

I landed with a grunt and smacked my lips as I tasted blood in my mouth from my bit cheek.

Who was the man who kept Samson on a leash? He had said only a word, yet it was enough to deter Samson. Was he the one known as Jesuit? I shivered in fear at the thought. Perhaps that was why they had defeated Micah and Savant so quickly.

As the boat moved I felt it began to angle upwards and as the boat breached the surface I saw that we were in some sort of cavern.

The man pressed a button and the hatch on the ceiling let out a *hiss* and rose open. Without looking at us he reached up, pulled down a ladder, climbed up, and left the boat.

Olympia rose and smiled at me. She strode over to me as Samson made his way to the ladder. She leaned in close until she was almost cheek to cheek and then spoke into my ear.

"Where did Odessa go?" Olympia whispered.

Her question shocked me. I did not know what her interest in Odessa was, but I could assume telling her would not be of any benefit to my friend. Perhaps I was not the bait as I had previously thought.

"I do not know," I lied. I tried to not break eye contact with her but after a couple seconds, I had to look away.

"Isn't it *vetiti* to lie?" Olympia said. She leaned back so I could see her smile. Her voice was heavy with charm, and she continued speaking.

It *was vetiti* to lie but telling Olympia where Odessa was could be a death sentence for her. I was already captured and there was no use in her being recaptured also.

"If you tell me where she went, I'll release your cuffs," she whispered.

I glanced behind Olympia at Samson who had paused on the ladder. He had an eyebrow raised in curiosity with a scowl on his face.

He caught me looking and sneered at me. He glanced at Olympia and began to descend the ladder and head our way.

Olympia punched me hard in the gut and I groaned in pain. It hurt but I knew she could have hurt me more if she had wanted to.

"Stay leaning," Olympia said through her teeth but the pain in my gut kept me from replying.

I felt Olympia click something on each of my cuffs. They hung loosely and if I had not been bent over, they would have loudly clanked on the metal floor of the boat.

"Quickly, now, tell me where Odessa is," Olympia said.

I hesitated once more. Samson was close. What would he do if I showed him Olympia had released me? The dynamic of the group led me to believe Samson was at the bottom of the hierarchy and making an enemy of Olympia did not seem like it would be beneficial.

"She is going to Pavrenes," I sighed.

Once Olympia heard my answer she stood up and about faced.

"Samson, stay here with the prisoners. I will join Hong Tao up ahead," she said and then climbed up the ladder and out of the boat leaving Samson behind with his jaw wide open.

His scowled deepened and he kicked a metal bin with his bare foot. He swore perhaps from the pain or maybe at the sight of the trash that covered the submarine floor.

I saw balled up sketches and letters and wondered if any of it could be important information. The sound had caused Savant to stir next to me, and Samson gave him a dirty look when he saw me looking.

I tried to not draw his attention further and hoped he would go sit up front, so I was grateful when Samson let out a huff and sat in the seat behind a small steering wheel.

I glanced at Savant and saw him blinking rapidly. He shook his head twice and then his head focused on me. He glanced at me, and I raised my wrist to show him that I was no longer cuffed.

Savant nodded his head and then gestured to Samson. I did not know what he was trying to communicate, and I wish I could hear his thoughts like I could with Odessa.

I carefully and silently removed the cuffs and placed them on the bench we sat on. I glanced at Samson once more before sliding as close to Savant as I could.

I inched my hand over Savant's body until I found his wrists. On the interior of each cuff, I found a switch that when triggered opened the yellow binds. I removed them before hiding them behind us in case Samson came over.

All that was left was Savant's back restraints. I glanced at Samson once more, but he was still stewing in his tantrum.

I gently pressed the release button on the strap that held Savant back on the bench. It let out a treacherous and thunderous *click* as the strap snapped back slamming into the metal wall we sat against with a large bang.

Micah stirred at the sound, and they were not the only one. Samson bolted up, turned around, and looked at me suspiciously.

"What are you up to over there?" he asked and when I did not answer he stood and began to approach me.

"What did Olympia say to you?" he asked.

His green eyes glistened like he was on the brink of tears, and he looked like a pitiful dog compared to the mighty lion that had tortured the people of Opulake days before.

"She asked me how someone as weak as me could defeat someone as strong as you; that you have gotten soft," I said, the lie leaving a sour taste in my mouth.

I spit the words and Samson growled but there was nothing he could do before Savant jumped up and slammed the palms of his hands down on each of Samson's ears.

His howl echoed throughout the boat, and I was sure that his allies would hear and come rushing to his aid.

But no one came and before Samson could react Savant coated his fist in his aura and slammed it into Samson's jaw. I heard an uncomfortable *pop* and Samson's body went slack as he crashed onto the floor.

Savant quickly removed the strap that held Micah back and removed their cuffs. Savant shook Micah gently until their eyes opened. Savant smiled and Micah smiled back although weakly.

"We got our butts handed to us," Micah said, and Savant nodded.

"What are we going to do?" I asked.

I looked through the glass to see if I could see the other bandits, but the window was opaque. I took a deep breath and waited for Savant to speak.

"We need to find out where we are and if possible, what the First Constellation are up to here," Savant said finally.

I shuddered. It did not seem like a promising idea to pursue the bandits after they had defeated us so easily. If we acted out again, they may not let us live.

We had the boat. We could bind Samson and just leave. Would that be so bad?

I thought of what Odessa would do. She would make sure her sister was safe, but I had no sister. Her home was her next priority, but I had no home.

She would not run; I knew that much. She would want to defeat all of the First Constellation and I had the opportunity to do that, excluding Jesuit.

I was just unsure that we *could* defeat them after Hong Tao, as Olympia had named him, had completely beat the Mystio.

Despite my doubts I kept my thoughts to myself. Olympia and Hong Tao were leaders in the First Constellation, and they were on my list.

Micah nodded.

"They caught me off guard last time; next time will be different," Micah said.

Savant released Micah and made sure they could steady themselves. Savant strode to the ladder and peered upwards.

"I'll go first, then you Arabella, and Micah will be in the rear," Savant said. "Any sign of our weapons?"

The three of us searched the boat for our weapons but it was in vain. Micah found a letter from the First Constellation boss Jesuit about an object they were searching for in the area but what the object was remained unclear.

I unrolled something that was wrapped in cloth and gasped as I recognized Odessa's sword scabbard. I had only seen it in her memories during our empathy link formation, but it was so unique I would recognize it anywhere.

Savant and Micah lifted Samson onto the bench. They combined two straps to keep him restrained. The cuffs did not look like they would fit but after pressing the release button the cuffs expanded open.

With the expanded cuffs Micah and Savant bound Samson's wrists and his ankles too with another pair of cuffs. It looked like Samson could break them easily, and I hope they had some sort of enchantment that would keep him restrained; after all, they had the power to block the use of magic.

After doing that with no weapons we lifted the hatch of the boat and slowly climbed up the metal ladder in the order Savant had instructed.

Savant reached his arm down, I gripped it, and he pulled me up. I looked around as I rose, and I gasped at the sight of the cavern.

"What is it?" Micah asked but I was speechless. I slid to the side so they could rise onto the top of the metal boat and Savant reached down to help Micah out too.

"Wow," Micah said as they emerged.

The roof of the cavern was coated with many spiked rocks that hung from the ceilings.

"Stalactites," Savant said. He too seemed to be in shock at the sight of the cavern.

"Are you sure they're not stalagmites?" Micah asked with a raised eyebrow and small smile.

"It's stalactites from the ceiling but there are some stalagmites over there?" Savant said pointing to the floor of the cave where more of the spikes rose from the ground as if they yearned for the spikes that reached down from the ceiling.

What was really amazing about the cavern was the ceiling which was illuminated by dots of glowing green light as if the light were growing on the rock itself.

"This," I said. "This is a sacred place."

Chapter FOUR

freya

A sacred place tainted by sinners.

I knew Olympia and Hong Tao were further in the cavern. In front of us I could see a tunnel that was also illuminated with the green lights that coated the ceiling and continued past the range of my vision.

Savant used his aura to form a bordeaux pathway from the boat's roof to the edge of the ground so we would not have to get wet from swimming over.

I thought about the similarities between Channeling and Elohan Faith Magic. Now that I had spent so much time around the Mystio I saw that it was not much different.

The main distinction in my head was that Channelers could not use the power of Eloah.

The most blessed Elohans in the world could be conduits to Eloah himself when he granted them his Blessing whereas Channelers were left to their own reserves.

The Blessing of Eloah was rare and most Elohans never reached the level of nirvana, devotion, or favor needed. It was something that my father had sought for his whole life but unless it came in Tyvent it was something that not even he achieved despite his dedication.

We made it to solid ground without incident and I glanced back towards where Samson was restrained. I wanted to make sure he was still restrained but it was in vain as I could not see him through the glass of the boat unfortunately.

Reluctantly, I followed Savant through the cavern tunnel. I was still opposed to the idea of exploring this unknown cave, but I figured it would be safer if we were all together.

With Micah as close as my shadow and Savant a few steps in front of me the three of us crept forward. Tears remained permanently at the edge of my eyes and fear clutched my heart tightly.

Arabella and the Tower of Magic

My heart raced and I had something like a headache as my anxiety kept my body in a constant state of fight or flight and flight was so close to winning.

We eased through the tunnel for an immeasurable amount of time while it seemed that the path was descending deeper and deeper into the planet.

I thought about Tachyon and Chalk Snout. I knew the horses would wait for us a bit before returning to the nearest Mystio hub, which in this case was Fort Mudo. That was if the First Constellation had not harmed them. I hoped they would be okay.

I wondered what kind of magic Hong Tao and Olympia could use. They had not demonstrated any forms of magic, just raw strength but perhaps in the case of Hong Tao he had magic that made him faster and stronger.

My negative thoughts had begun to swell, and I wondered how far the path went and if Samson was still unconscious and when we would run into the First Constellation.

The thoughts occupied me so much that when the path began to blossom open I did not notice it until I reached a drop at the end of the path that revealed a chasm below us.

In the chasm were the ruins of a great city of stone. Opulake had been a small town and although Drie and South Dresden were much larger than Opulake, the city below seemed to surpass it as if it could have housed over a hundred thousand people.

Despite its size and potential, the city was dark and completely empty without a hint of movement or life. It seemed haunted or cursed and despite its vast size I was only more afraid at its appearance even though I saw no signs of Hong Tao or Olympia.

Its stone buildings were composed of black metals and green stones. As we descended a set of steep and long stairs towards the city and saw that many of the buildings were lined with gems and gold trimmings.

Just one of those gems could have me living the rest of my life happy and on permanent vacation but who would I spend those days with?

There was no one.

"What is this place?" I asked the Mystio.

"I do not know for sure, but judging by the architecture I believe this is one of the old dwarven cities," Savant said. "How it ended up down here I do not know."

A dwarven city? They were long gone but if one had been preserved like this one had it would be a testament of history. It was amazing that someone as insignificant as me could be a part of this historical greatness.

"After the Battle of the Sojourners, it was said that a great wave came from the east and washed away the armies of humans and dwarves," Savant continued. "It's possible that this is one of those cities. I don't know much about Dwarven Era History, the Queen has restricted much about them and the kings of that era," Savant finished.

"I wish Adonis was here, he knew much more than us about the dwarves," Micah said. "I believe this city was called Jormondor. It was the dwarven capital. You're right though, Lancer Solace, the battle had actually been won by the dwarves but after the battle a tsunami came in and washed most of the dwarves away."

It was fascinating that so much history had been right under my nose. I wonder what Odessa would say. The island she lived on was not far from here. Did she know that this great city lay under the sea so close to her?

She would still be on the road I knew, and I hoped she, Talicia, and Adonis were safe wherever they were at.

I once again considered reaching out to her with our empathy link, but I was still low on magic from our beach skirmish and there still may have been fighting left to take part in.

I would need that magic even though speaking to her would probably put my mind at ease. I knew she would have words of encouragement for me that would make this easier.

Jormondor was so quiet. It was unsettling. I felt like I could hear everyone's heartbeat and it made me feel uneasy.

Perhaps this place was abandoned for a reason, I wanted to say, but Savant suddenly held up his hand and Micah and I halted. I looked but I did not see anything that called for a halt until I heard a woman nearby crying softly.

Savant knelt and leaned around the corner of the closest building. I crouched behind her, and I saw not Olympia but a woman.

Her pale blue eyes were full of tears and even though Savant had only peaked around the corner she saw him and cried out for help.

Savant quickly looked both ways as he checked our surroundings for trouble.

"Micah, stay here with Arabella, watch for trouble, three note whistle," Savant said.

"Heard," Micah said and after that Savant rushed towards the girl.

He gestured to her to calm down and after a moment she did. They spoke in rushed whispers that I could not discern what they were saying.

I watched as Savant helped her sit up and as he let out a low two note whistle Micah pulled me forward. We arrived at the girl, and I was able to get a better look at her freckled face.

She looked a bit older than me, but she was still in her early twenties with orange hair like autumn leaves. She wore an elaborate blue and gold sleeveless robe that let me know she or someone she had a relation with was very important as the robes were quite expensive.

"Micah, she has a wound on her head, can you tend to it," Savant asked.

Micah nodded and they Channeled their aura. They gingerly placed their hand on the girl's head. Micah found the wound as a wince of pain came from the girl and began to work on it with their magic.

"We are not the best healers," Savant explained. "It is not a skill I possess, and it's not Micah's forte either."

I wanted to ask Savant more about it. The art of healing with magic was not rare but it was not common either, but before I could he began talking to the girl.

"Who are you?" Savant asked. "What are you doing here?" His head swiveled in all directions making sure we remained safe where we were.

"My name is Freya Lunaredi, daughter of Fulla Lunaredi," she said. "I'm here looking for—"

She stopped speaking as the tallest tower of Jormondor lit up at the top as if a signal had been set ablaze and then the black metal of the tower began to turn gold.

The light at the top was like a watch tower and multiple beams of light shone down throughout the town as if they were searching for something.

"Hide!" Savant hissed.

Micah and Savant grabbed the arms of the girl and pulled her into a thin alley to the right and instead of waiting I rolled left into another alley.

Just as I cleared the street a beam of light shined down and up the street. I brushed myself off and peeked my head from around the wall.

I saw the gold oozing upward from the base of the tower as if it was some gravity defying liquid and began to completely coat the black metal of the tower as it reached for the tip at the top.

I had a feeling that Olympia and Hong Tao were up there, they had found what they had come for, and that we were too late. We should have retreated.

I looked towards Savant to let him know this but as I looked across the street, I saw that he along with Micah and Freya were gone.

I am alone.

They had left me.

I did not have much time to panic over their vanishing because as the panic began to set in the ground began to shake, and a large crack ruptured at my feet.

I attempted to jump but the ground gave way underneath me. I tried to grab the ledge of the street with my fingers and then with my Faith, but my fingers could not reach, and I was not able to meld my Faith into something that could grip the ledge and catch me under distress.

I was plunged into darkness and the green lights that lit the world above vanished. I fell for only a few seconds, but it seemed longer and when the ground came, I was almost surprised.

The force of the fall drove all the air out of my lungs in a tremendous gasp and for a moment I lay there inhaling and exhaling quickly and in pain without moving.

I would have laid there longer if not for the sound of something moving in the darkness. I froze and held my breath.

Had it been a rock or something else falling from the quake? I listened hard urging my ears to expand but I could not hear the sound anymore.

I felt uneasy and said a prayer of safety to Eloah and then after steeling my nerves I stood up. I focused on my Faith and lit my hand with my aura.

Holding up my hand I was able to illuminate the area some like a weak torch, but it was better than being left in the paranoia of darkness.

I looked and saw the hole I had fallen from some thirty feet up. I attempted climb back up, but the rock was black and slimy. The slime smelled smoky and kept me from getting a good grip.

After my third try, I had managed to climb several feet but once again I heard something shifting in the darkness behind me.

I turned my head quickly and the motion caused me to lose my grip and I fell once more. This time I landed hard on my butt and the failure brought tears to my eyes.

I was very low on magic and the longer I kept the pit lit with my aura the less magic I was left with. I dared not yell for help as I did not want to draw the wrong attention, but I needed help. I thought once more of Odessa and our empathy link.

Now was the kind of emergency that was appropriate to request some of her magic; after all, she had much more magic than I did.

I knelt onto my knees, braced myself for the coming darkness, and let my Faith fade away. I took a deep breath to steady myself and closed my eyes. Even though I was already in darkness, closing my eyes helped me focus.

Extending the tendrils of my mind I reached for the mind of Odessa so that I could speak with her but when I projected myself onto Odessa's mind. Unfortunately, it was not there to catch mine like it should have been.

It was a bad omen. It either meant we were too far from each other or that one or both of us were out of magic.

Neither thought was very comforting as a lack of magic meant she was fighting heavily, and the long distance made no sense unless I was much deeper underground than I thought.

I wondered if it had anything to do with this ancient city. It was a dwarven city and perhaps they had a method to prevent the use of some types of magic.

I stood and stomped my boot in frustration. Once more I looked upwards and attempted to climb the rock face. This time instead of purely using the rock I attempted to use my Faith to reinforce my feet to give me better footholds.

It helped but by doing so with my limited magic I was not able to see around me as well and just focused on the green light that I could now see leaking from the hole above.

It was slow going and although I slipped twice, I was able to regain my balance with the Faith I had sent to my feet.

I had almost reached the top when I heard the sound of something scuttling to my left. I froze and looked to my left but saw nothing.

Suddenly the sound came from the right and it was much closer this time. Something was definitely there, watching me in the darkness.

I wondered what it was and what it was waiting for. After all, I had been in the hole for several minutes. I contemplated lashing out in an attempt to scare the creature, but I did not have the energy to maintain my position and stall so instead I focused on escaping the hole.

I exhaled deeply and wiped the sweat from my forehead with my wrist. With an almighty push I focused my Faith under my feet and lifted a feeble construct that wobbled and shattered quickly but it was enough to raise me to the lip of the street I'd fallen from.

I leaned both of my elbows on the street and gradually pulled myself upwards. I stood slowly and leaned on my knees.

I looked across the street to where the Mystio had been with the orange haired woman, but they were still missing.

I wondered if the woman was part of the First Constellation, left there as a trap. Where could they have gone? Did she have something to do with the quake?

I glanced upwards at the glowing tower that was now completely gold and figured that was the place to go next. I would find either the First Constellation or the Mystio there.

I was now truly alone, no one could stop me from leaving now. I could probably figure out the metal boat, but I could not leave the Mystio stranded after they had done so much for me.

Samson was still free.

I brushed off my clothing and exhaled deeply. I said a prayer of strength but as I attempted to move forward, I found that my feet were caught up in some sort of sticky substance. I had no idea how or when it had happened.

It looked like spider webs but glowed with a ghostly whiteness. My feet and up to my calves were restrained in the substance and any attempt to free myself only made me wobble.

I looked frantically for whatever had restrained me. I had seen spiders before in my life, but none could create such strong and large webs so quickly; after all, I had only looked away for a moment.

Just at the corner of my eyesight I saw the leg of the creature. It shifted as I moved my head, always staying at the edge of my perception.

I feinted my head right and then quickly shifted my head left and I caught full sight of the creature before it could hide.

It was not quite a spider as it had eight legs along with a set of claws. It had a metallic exoskeleton that reflected the light of the green that glowed from the ceiling.

It was also much larger than the largest spider thing I had ever seen. The creature was the size of the average dog. It almost seemed to glow and was so vibrant and dazzling I was surprised I had not seen the creature before now, even in the dimness of the chasm.

"Hey there," I said with my hands up.

Perhaps the creature could understand me, and if it could, perhaps I could communicate with it and talk my way out of it.

If it did not I steeled myself for a fight. I felt semi confident that I could win. I had been meditating and watching as everyone around me used magic. I should have been able to take it down, after all, it was only one creature.

As the thought crossed my mind the creature climbed on the street along with two other creatures. My heart plummeted and as the creatures' jaws let out a *clink* sound from their mouths and snouts emerged that were pointed like spears.

I lifted my arms and brought forth my Faith. The closest creature chirped and then it jumped onto my left arm. I attempted to swat at it but before I was able to another jumped onto my other arm.

I began to cry out as the first creature bit into my left arm. As it did so I could feel my Faith draining. It was absorbing my magic!

The third eased forward and I watched as it bent its knees slowly and then it jumped, and its legs wrapped themselves around my head.

The legs tightened around my head and then it bit hard, and every drop of magic left my body.

Chapter FIVE

gorin

I was trapped as a summer fly in the web of a red ember spider.

I grappled at the legs of the spider creatures and for my struggles the claws of the creatures snapped at my hands drawing blood.

My hands began to sting from the cuts, and I felt blood beginning to pool in my palms. My eyes began to water, and tears rolled down my cheeks. I knew there was much of me to eat, and I worried more of the creatures would appear.

I could not just let them kill me. I could not die. The creature on my face obstructed my view and I gripped a leg on either side of its body.

I tightened my hands and attempted to infuse the maneuver with my Faith to make me stronger, but only a faint manifestation of my Faith appeared.

The creatures had latched onto my arms, adding weight that made it harder to maneuver them. With a grunt, I began to pull, and I pulled until each leg stretched to the point where they began to tear and creak with a sound like metal hinges that desperately needed to be oiled.

Gold liquid flowed from the wound and onto my clothes. The liquid was like boiling water, and I cried out and released the creature as it poured on me.

My dress began to steam and after pulling the sleeves to cover my hands I began to wipe the liquid off of me and onto the ground.

The damaged creature fell to the ground with a rough cracking sound and did not move any further. I exhaled deeply and reached for the next creature that was still plunged in my left arm.

I gripped the claw arm and pulled. My arm cried and I could feel the creature's snout moving through my skin as I yanked.

The arm creaked off and more of the gold liquid leaked from the wound. This time I expected it, and I aimed it onto the webs that still restrained my feet.

It scorched my bare feet but as the liquid flowed away the webs decomposed and the liquid carried away what remained of them. I repeated the maneuver with the final spider creature and aimed its bodily fluids onto the street.

Free from the creatures I was going to proceed towards the golden tower when I heard a loud whistling sound from the hole I had climbed out of. I looked down and saw the Mystio Micah.

They were there surrounded by even more spiders than I had been and even from where I stood, I could see burns along their skin. There was no sign of the others, and I wondered if it was a trap of some kind set by the First Constellation.

Shaking off the thought I called down to them that I would be down to assist them as quickly as I could although I felt extremely nauseous and could taste vomit in my mouth.

I was burned, bloody, and exhausted but there was no Estella here to help me; no Odessa here to save me; no Tripa Fons here to guide me.

I feared running into Samson or Hong Tao alone. I did not have the power necessary to defeat them on my own.

"I am so tired," I said aloud, although there was no one there to hear it, and before I knew it, I was in the realm of dreams.

o

Arabella and the Tower of Magic

I had a dream about Estella.

Although I am not sure if it could have been considered a dream as she was only there for a moment before fading away.

She had twisted her daggers causing them to spin in her palms and then with her left dagger she had pointed to a lake with an island in the middle and then she was gone, and I was awake.

I stood up shakily and the first thing I noticed was the Mystio next to me. Micah was unconscious once more and clutching their arm.

Their skin was coated in burns, and I imagined they had come into contact with the spider creatures, but the number of burns made me think that they had fought off many more than I had.

The second thing I noticed was the source of the light where I was. On the ceiling was a large gem of some sort that exuded a radiant light.

It gave off no fire like our torches and I sat up and reached for it. It gave off no heat but before I could touch it a raspy voice spoke from behind saying, "Touch that I would not."

I turned around quickly and saw a short woman with long brown hair that cascaded down her shoulders. Her skin was rough and muscular, yet her face was rounded and surrounded by dark blue eyes.

I reached for a weapon, but I had none. Odessa's scabbard was empty. I wished I had maintained one of the metal creature's claws. It would have been better than nothing.

"Why not?" I asked glancing at the large glowing gem once more. Its light spread throughout the room we were in, and I noticed a creature of some sort.

It resembled a large dog, but it was made of some sort of black metal. It was relaxed, laying on its stomach as if it was napping but its glowing orange eyes watched me intently.

Black smoke puffed out of its nostrils, and I marveled at its existence. I had never seen a living creature made of metal although I had heard legends of them.

"You search for *imperi,* do you not? Behold, there it is. Touch it and be transported to a world of goblins and daysleepers," the stranger said, her eyes looking deep into mine.

"No, I am not looking for *imperi*, only my friends and the fiends known as the First Constellation," I replied levelly.

"There are no fiends in this realm, I know that much has not changed at least," the woman said. She was quiet for a minute as I waited for her to give more information about herself, and she burst out in a fit of laughter.

"Oh, was that a joke?" I asked letting out a nervous chuckle.

"Yes, yes it was," she said. "That is no *imperi,* only a light gem. No human would know the difference though and you are not the first to come searching for our power."

"You are a dwarf," I asked but my tone was that of a statement.

"I am what remains of one, yes. I was old when this city was engulfed by the Great Ocean and now, I am even older," she said.

She stood on the tips of her toes, arched her back, and stretched her arms until I heard her back pop and she sighed in relief.

"I am not here searching for power," I replied. "I am looking for the First Constellation lieutenant leaders. One is a woman named Olympia and the other is named Hong Tao. Have you seen or heard of either of them?"

The dwarven woman laughed and Micah stirred next to me. Their golden brown eyes revealed themselves and I saw them take in where we were and what our situation might be, which I myself did not yet know.

"I can see you yearn for power; it is clear in your spirit. But no, I have not encountered the humans you have described," she answered.

I sighed in frustration. I was interested in the dwarven woman, I had never met one before, but I did not have a lot of time to waste learning lore and what her words meant.

I offered my arm to Micah, and they gripped it so they could stand and leaned onto my shoulder while they caught their breath.

"What is your name? Who are you? Where is the *imperi* located?" Micah asked in between heavy breaths.

The woman smiled at their questions. She straightened her back before speaking, although it did not do much to raise her stature.

"I am Lady Gorin, partner to Lady Kuri, daughter of Lady Glorid of the Duskdelver Clan and the last Guardian of Jormondor," she said with apparent pride. "Who are you?"

"Arabella, of Opulake," I replied looking up once more at the light gem.

"And I—", Micah started and then straightened their back, bowed their head slightly, and said "I am Pershing Micah of Jemny."

Lady Gorin frowned and said, "I have always hated how humans are so picky about who gets a title, or surname. It makes it hard to make connections for those of us who live much longer. I am not familiar with the human settlements of Opulake or Jemny."

"Sorry," I apologized on the behalf of all humans and then asked, "What are you doing here, Lady Gorin?"

"I have guarded the *imperi* of Jormondor for decades, but lately I have been focusing on this replica of the city."

She gestured to the wall, and I saw a stone replica of Jormondor that was being carved directly out of the cavern wall.

Micah approached it slowly, yet I could see the interest on their face. They leaned over the replica and took in every detail.

I guessed it was like a map and they were doing it for information yet all they said was "This is so amazing."

Its details were immaculate, and I could tell it had taken a lot of time. I could see furniture through the windows of the building. Perhaps it had taken decades and I could tell the carving was an art that took a lot of time to keep accurate.

As I had knelt over to inspect the city, Lady Gorin strode over to me and snatched Odessa's scabbard off of my back.

"Hey!" I said as I stood up quickly and reached for the scabbard in Lady Gorin's hands. Micah was instantly alert with their hands ready to fight if needed but they hesitated.

"This is dwarven made, where did you get this?" she asked as she studied the glyphs on the surface of the scabbard.

"It belongs to a woman named Odessa, but it was stolen by the First Constellation. She is my friend and I mean to return it to her," I said with my hand out for the scabbard.

"Odessa. Hmm. It is not a dwarven name. Does she not have a clan name? What of her lineage?" Lady Gorin asked holding the scabbard directly under the glow of the light gem.

"I believe it is just Odessa of Pavrenes. Her father's name is Grimke, but I do not remember her mother's name."

"Yet she is your friend?" Lady Gorin said with a raised eyebrow.

"She saved my life, so yes," I replied.

"This scabbard belongs to the sword of the High King Potiphar, *Prern*. Is this Odessa you speak of here with you?" Lady Gorin said as she finally placed the scabbard in my hand.

I gripped it and then tied it back onto my back.

"No," I said lowering my arms. "She has gone back to Pavrenes."

"You might not tell others that so quickly," Micah said their face in a wince.

They were right of course. I had stressed so much over whether I should tell Olympia about Odessa's destination, yet I had let it slip so easily with Lady Gorin.

I vowed to be more tight lipped but it was just something about Lady Gorin that made her seem familiar to me. I felt that I could trust her, but I knew it was foolish to trust her so easily. Yet the feeling persisted.

"I am not familiar with this Pavrenes either," Lady Gorin admitted.

I smiled at her.

"You may need to get out just a bit more. Pavrenes is a small settlement nearby. It lies to the east on an unnamed island. Opulake is to the west and Jemny to the northwest."

Lady Gorin approached us with a clear jar filled with something that looked like dark green clay. She approached Micah who hesitated and then nodded their head in consent.

Lady Gorin spread the clay along Micah's wounds and along their wounded arm and then repeated the process with me.

The clay smelled musty and felt cold like ice. I enjoyed the cold feeling but after several seconds it transitioned into a burning sensation. The burning was only temporary and after it faded my body felt free of any injuries.

My exhaustion and magic fatigue persisted but my body felt better than it had in over a month.

"I thank you for healing and mending us," Micah said bowing their head once more and I mimicked their gesture.

"If you guard the *imperi* you can come help us stop the First Constellation!" I said smiling widely at Lady Gorin. "After that, I could take you to Odessa."

"Pah!" Lady Gorin said. "I care no longer for that cursed object. Our last defense of that blasted ring led to the descent of my life partner. It was not a satisfactory exchange. I will give no more."

I took a moment to compose my words, as I knew I would only have one attempt to win her over, and I did not want to disrespect her fallen life partner.

"If we do not prevent the First Constellation from acquiring the *imperi* hundreds more will descend. We, *I* need your help. I could even talk to Lancer Savant Solace about rewarding you. We could get you out of this city too."

I looked to Micah for back up, but they were silent.

"You guys could reward her, right?" I asked them, extending a request for reassurance.

Your ignorance is showing, human," Lady Gorin said, and the metal dog lifted its head and its orange eyes glowed brighter.

"Only a true dwarf could descend. You humans keep your heaven in the sky. I am no rat trapped in a cage this is my home. I could leave at any time. How could a human reward me with anything from their stolen realm. Anything they could offer me would already be mine birthright."

"Lady Gorin, please. These people, these murderers have killed everyone I have ever loved and without you they will kill many more."

Lady Gorin's metallic clothing seemed to shimmer as she turned to face me.

"Begone from me, Arabella of Opulake. You humans, *you* murderers have killed everyone *I* have ever loved. Begone!"

"Lady—" I started but Lady Gorin placed her left palm over the bracelet on her right wrist and the metal beast rose and pounced towards me.

"This is Canus," Lady Gorin said.

"Arabella!" Micah called.

I knew they were weak as I was from the spider creatures draining our magic, yet they managed an aura construct that wrapped around the metal beast and threw it backwards.

Lady Gorin rushed towards Micah and threw a handful of blue powder that turned into smoke. Micah breathed it in, and they fell towards the ground.

I rolled over quickly and caught them, preventing their head from hitting the ground but before I could react, Lady Gorin clouded my face with the blue smoke.

A sweet smelling scent emanated, and I attempted to not breathe, but it was in vain as I felt my senses beginning to fade.

"Please," I uttered once before my mind was snuffed once more.

Chapter SIX

hua

My vision returned blurry and at first sight I could have sworn the person leaning over me was Hong Tao.

I yelled and slid backwards. This person had the same golden brown skin and brown hair but as my vision focused, I saw that it was a woman, not a man.

"Lady Gorin?" I mumbled, my eyes searching for the dwarven woman, but she was gone.

"You're lucky to be alive, aren't ya?" the brown haired woman said with a concerned expression. She held both hands up in front of her asking me to calm down.

I exhaled deeply and then turned over onto my stomach and retched on the ground. I was coated in blood, slime, and dirt.

The stench of my own throw up forced itself up my nostrils and overwhelmed my sense of smell. I felt absolutely disgusting.

The woman had stood and backed away at my sudden movement and she watched from a safe distance with a look of sympathy on her face.

Once my breakfast and the previous day's dinner had been expunged from my stomach, I pulled myself onto my knees and forced myself to get out of the area of filth.

I stunk, I could smell it and I knew she did too so when I stood up and approached the woman, I didn't get too close to her.

Micah was also stirring next to the corpses of the spider creatures all around me motionless on the ground. It appeared somehow Lady Gorin had left us where I had been before I had fainted at the edge of the pit I had climbed out of.

As Micah rose, I knelt next to one of the spiders intending to inspect it but a flash of lightning on the inside shocked me and I jumped back.

I stepped onto the corpse of one of the spider creatures with a *crunch* and almost fell back into the mixture of blood, throw up, and the bodily fluids of the creatures. It looked like the creatures had no flesh in them and were completely composed of metal and lightning.

I wondered if they too had been constructed by Lady Gorin and the other dwarves or if perhaps they existed as the inspiration for the golems.

The woman was watching me silently. I took a deep breath as I composed myself and then looked into her brown eyes.

"Who are you?" I asked.

"My name is Hua Li. Your next question is probably, what are you doing here, ain't it? The answer to that is that I am here searching for my father, have you seen him?"

"Your father?" I said with the feeling of sickliness returning to my stomach even though I had nothing else to hurl.

"Yes, his name is Hong Tao Li, one of the lieutenants in the bandit group known as the First Constellation, have you seen him?"

I took a step back and Micah moved in front of me as I attempted to manifest my Faith but save for a few sparks of neon green my Faith remained dormant.

The spider creatures had drained all of my magic, but I had hoped some had recovered by now. I had very low magic reserves to begin with and my magic recovery was slow.

I knew there was something off about Hua, and not just because she ended every statement like a question. She was an enemy talking to me like we were strangers at the market.

"Woah," Hua said raising her hands at the sight of the green sparks from mine. There ain't no need for magic, is there?"

"There is if you're with the First Constellation," I said.

"I'm not here to *help* my father. I'm here to *kill* him; did you know that?"

"Do you know where your father is?" Micah asked her and she nodded.

"Kill him?" I said. "Why would you want to kill him?

I relaxed some at her words, but after Lady Gorin's switch up I did not want to take any chances. My eyes continued to search for the rest of my party. Where were Savant and Freya? How many others were in Jormondor?

I also remained wary of the First Constellation leaders and more of those silver spider creatures. I could not afford to be caught off guard again.

"I am my mother's onryō, don't ya know?" she said. "He is here in this city searching for an *imperi*."

Onryō were wrathful spirits. I did not know much about them but as far as I understood it, they were similar to banshees. Banshees were the spirits of Channelers who died while Channeling large amounts of magic. As they magic became sentient and left an imprint on the world.

The thing about onryō and banshees was that they were both dead and Hua looked very much alive. I could not imagine being placed in a position to where I would have to kill either of my parents.

I resented them a lot for leaving me alone in Opulake without any other family, but they like many Elohans considered other Elohans family. Despite my resentment I could never imagine them doing anything where my recourse would be murder.

"If you're here to kill Hong Tao, we're on the same side," Micah said.

I was not so sure of the certainty of their statement, but I had heard of the saying that "the enemy of my enemy is my friend."

I did not like her relation to Hong Tao, but it was true that Odessa and I had been strangers before we worked together in Opulake.

Against my better judgement I decided to trust Hua. After all, she could not help who her parents were.

Perhaps we would end this adventure as friends, as Odessa and I had done.

"Aw, you are Mystio?" Hua asked, studying Micah's uniform.

I took note of how she spat the word "Mystio" and the expression of distaste that crossed her face when she said it.

"Yes, we were captured," Micah explained and smiled embarrassingly.

Hua nodded her head but did not inquire further.

"And what's your name?" Hua asked me and I considered lying but chose otherwise.

"Arabella of Opulake, at your service," I said.

As I said the words, I remembered how I had said them to Odessa when I had first met her. The fact that I had not been able to reach her was worrisome.

"And I am Pershing Micah," Micah said. "As Arabella said we came here to stop the First Constellation leaders. We were separated from my lancer, Lancer Savant Solace and a girl we found down here."

"You said you saw a woman here? What did she look like? Did you see a man also?" Hua inquired and I wondered if and how she knew Freya Lunaredi.

"We did meet a woman. She had red hair and blue eyes, and her name was Freya. She should still be with Lancer Solace, but we didn't find a man," Micah answered. "We were split from them during the quake."

"I came here with Freya, but my boyfriend was also with us. His name is Frey. We somehow ended up separated with the spell that brought us here."

I wondered what kind of magic allowed them to travel here without a boat or any normal travel. Although I could not think of what normal form of travel *could* get someone here. Even the metal underwater boat was abnormal in my opinion.

"I haven't seen anyone else down here but you and a girl named Freya. Frey and Freya though, isn't that a coincidence?" Micah asked with a small smile.

Hua groaned.

"Freya is his overbearing twin sister, she insisted on coming with us but the *imperi* is small, it got us here, but we were all split up, does that make sense?"

"Wait, you have an *imperi,* a real *imperi*?" I asked.

"You have an *imperi* but you're *not* with the First Constellation?" Micah asked, their face skeptical.

"Right, any other questions?" Hua asked, not impolitely.

"How did you come about an *imperi*?" Micah inquired.

"I—" Hua started. "I don't remember, isn't that weird?"

Micah raised an eyebrow, but they did not push the subject, and when neither they nor I said anything, Hua continued speaking.

"It is very small and almost out of power. That is how we got split up and it really only has two more trips worth of magic at the most. You won't get any funny ideas, will you?" Hua said with a smile and held up a ring.

The ring was made of a black metal, and it had a black gem on the face. It was a wonderous gem, and although it was black it shined with the light of a hundred colors.

"That is how you arrived here?" I asked and Hua nodded her head.

My eyes were drawn to the *imperi's* gemstone. It looked like the white opals we had in Churches of Eloah but instead of a white base its base was black, and the difference made the colors all the more vibrant.

I felt drawn to it and lifted my hand slightly and then halted it. I forced myself to look away from the *imperi* and I saw both Micah and Hua watching me closely.

"Savant Solace?" Hua asked. "Any relation to Verdant Solace?"

"Verdant is his older brother," Micah said, and I took note of the information. In our brief time together, I had learned extraordinarily little about the personal lives of Micah and Savant.

"We should go to the tower," Hua said, gesturing to the golden tower. "That's where my father will be, don't you think?"

I nodded my head.

"After you," I said and together we began to climb the stairs towards the shining tower.

o

We arrived at the base of the tower without incident, but I was disappointed to see a metal door at the base.

The door seemed airtight with nowhere to open, and it seemed we had come all this way for no reason. I wondered if we could climb it from the outside and reach the tower roof that way.

Hua saw my face and smiled.

"Not worried, are you?" she said, and she approached that tower door and studied it. After a moment she pressed the ring into an impression and the door shifted and opened with a loud *click*.

"I left it open in case the others get here after us. I'm assuming my father is already up above us, don't you see the gold?"

"How did you get here if not by *imperi*?" Hua asked us as we approached the doorway at the base of the tower.

"We were captured by the First Constellation, and they brought us here in some sort of underwater boat," I said.

Hua nodded her head.

"It's called a submarine. They allow people to go under water for a brief amount of time," she said. "Very useful, but very dangerous, don't you think?"

I had never heard of boats that could go underwater. It was amazing that such technology existed.

I turned and studied the city once more. From where we stood, I could see nearly the entirety of the dark city.

I was searching for any signs of movement that might reveal the others but the world below me remained motionless. I saw no life although I knew it was there.

I glanced upwards at the tower of gold and saw just how high it went. It was at least twice as high as the Opulaki Aid Tower and I was sure the former lord of Opulake, Laurens, would have appreciated the view.

I could hear the sound of gears turning and the sound of metal from within the walls. The walls themselves were made of the same gold metal and were covered in etchings.

I sighed as I passed through the doorway of the tower with my stomach full of butterflies. We had made it through the city without encountering the First Constellation, but that only meant they would be here, and I did not look forward to our rematch.

I leaned in close to inspect the etchings and drawings on the walls. I saw the scene of what I assumed was a dwarf climbing out of the ground, there was another scene of a dwarf being thrown by a giant, and another scene of dwarves with their weapons drawn on the shore of a beach as a boat with other people on it approached.

I wanted to inspect the giant more and look for other depictions of them but before I could I heard a sound at the door.

I turned quickly, using my Faith to coat my knuckles for both offense and defense. It was a thin coating, but the neon green magic was slowly returning to my body.

"Stand down it's just Frey, don't you see?" Hua said with a wide smile that showed off her brilliant white teeth.

Frey was tall and slender although not as tall as Samson with very pale blond hair that was bald on the sides like Micah's but was a bit shorter on the top.

He wore a premium sleeveless robe like the one his sister Freya had worn, and it was blue like hers had been, but it was slightly darker.

Although they had different hair colors and Frey lacked the freckles that were splattered across Freya's face they shared the same pale blue eyes.

Hua wrapped her arms around Frey tightly and they shared the same pale blue eyes,pulled him in close. Frey hugged her back, but he shifted his hands across her torso as if he was unsure where to put them.

"Who is that?" I heard him whisper.

"This is Arabella, did you know she's from Opulake?" Hua said introducing me.

"I'm sorry about what happened to your home," Frey said.

He had a much softer voice than I had expected for someone so tall. I thought he probably had a great singing voice.

"Has news spread of its destruction already?" I asked.

I knew Savant had sent off pigeons, but I didn't think to meet anyone who had heard of the Opulaki Massacre by the First Constellation yet.

Frey blushed before speaking.

"Maybe, I'm not sure. We passed through it on the way here," he said softly.

If that was the case, they must have been right behind us because we had just left Opulake before being abducted.

It was at that point that I wondered how long we had been unconscious. It had only felt like minutes, but it might have been hours, perhaps days.

"Did you see any others out there?" I asked.

"Others?" Frey said and that was answer enough but I clarified anyway.

"Yes, a Mystio. We came here with them, but we got split up. Your sister, Freya, was also last seen with him," Micah said.

"Maybe we should go find them," Frey said hesitantly, looking from the stairs of the tower to the city below and behind us.

I agreed with his sentiment. Savant was probably our strongest fighter. I did not know how strong Frey and Hua were, but I figured we had the best chance of victory with Savant's help and even Freya's too; we needed all the help we could get.

Hua shook her head.

"This is Jormondor. It was one of the largest dwarven cities, we don't have the time to look for them, do you hear me?" Hua said.

I was unsure if speed was more important than strength, but the tower *had* been lit for quite a while. Whatever Olympia and Hong Tao were after would be bad news for anyone else, and I knew Savant intended to prevent this from happening.

But Savant was not here.

Only Eloah could take my life for his cause, and I could not just risk my life in vain. My life was linked with Odessa's.

I told myself that thinking we should flee and run back to the submarine was not cowardice, simply smart thinking. It was a tactical retreat. We would be back.

The Queen had a whole army and despite the strength of the Mystio and their legends it seemed Hong Tao was just more powerful, even without the use of magic. His strength made me shiver at the thought of Hong Tao's leader, Jesuit, who in theory would be even stronger.

If Jesuit took a submarine here as the other members had we would be dead, and it would be so easy for our enemy to achieve it. Then there was still Olympia who had yet to fight but I knew she must have some power of her own to reach such a high rank in the bandit organization.

I was just about to voice my thoughts to Hua and Frey when a voice came from the door. I looked over and despite everything I sighed in relief.

"Aw, you waited," Savant said with a smile. "You shouldn't have."

Chapter SEVEN

frey

Eloah be blessed, Savant was not alone.

Next to him was Freya and the two of them looked as if they had been fighting as hard as I had.

Savant's cape was in tatters and Freya's blue robe was so filthy and now all its vibrancy had been replaced with blackness and filth.

Savant nodded his head at me and then studied both Hua and Frey.

"Savant, these are Hua and Frey," I said introducing them. "Hua, Frey, this is Savant, another Mystio."

"We're here for Hong Tao, the First Constellation leader," Hua said evenly. "I'm no fan of the Damasyri military, but currently we have the same goal, don't you think?"

Savant nodded his head and studied the walls of the tower, and I could not help but grin. Everyone was here. We might have a chance now.

Freya walked over to Frey and the closer she got the smaller he appeared and when she was in range, she slapped him on the back of the head.

"Hey!" Hua said. "There's no need for that, is there?"

"I guess I deserved that," Frey said sheepishly as he rubbed the back of his head to ease the sting.

"That and more," Freya said.

With them both in better light I saw that the tips of each of their ears were tipped like fairies. I wondered if they were descendants or if it was just a mutation.

"The First Constellation is up above?" Savant asked, looking at me and ignoring the scene between the siblings.

"Yes," Hua said before I could answer.

"We stand together," Savant said. "I do not know the specifics of your being here but if you plan to help us fight the First Constellation the details can wait until after. Are we ready?"

I had meditated to regain some magic, but my magical reserves were still low. I doubted we could afford to wait longer so I simply nodded my head.

Savant led the way up the stairs with Hua, Frey, and Freya following in that order leaving Micah and I alone for a moment.

I glanced at Micah hesitantly, but with a smile they gestured that I should go before them, so I did, and they guarded our rear.

Rings that held streams of red lightning illuminated our way. They were dotted in abundance along the walls and ceiling. I had never seen such technology or magic. Truly some things the dwarves had created must have been lost with them.

I heard a commotion up ahead but all I could see was shadow and darkness. I quickened my pace, but I could only go as fast as Freya allowed me to as she was blocking my path.

I heard growling and as I passed through the veil of shadow, I said a prayer of safety for myself and the others.

The shadow felt ice cold, colder than anything I had ever felt. My entire body was covered in goosebumps and my hair straightened and stood at attention.

I blinked hard and saw the others on the defensive against two large creatures of darkness. The Mystio were weaponless, but the others were armed.

Freya wielded a whip that snapped at the shadow beasts. Frey held a wooden quarter staff that I had somehow not noticed before now that was made of a light colored wood. Hua wielded a staff made of a similar wood but hers was able to separate into three pieces connected by a cord of some sort.

The creatures seemed to be made of shadow themselves and they shifted from incorporeal and physical forms.

Their spiritual forms were composed of wisps of smoke, and they had glowing orange eyes that shifted across their heads in constant movement.

When the shadow beasts shifted to their physical forms they appeared as large muscular dogs with sharp teeth. Saliva oozed from their maw and their eyes appeared as burning embers but did not move as they did in their shadow form.

"Hell hounds," I heard Micah say behind me.

I had heard of hell hounds, but never seen them. They were created with blood through a spell that was part Shadow Magic, part Blood Magic, and I wondered if it was Olympia or Hong Tao that had summoned them.

The larger of the hell hounds was engaged with Savant and Hua, along with Frey who watched them close by. The hound gnashed at Savant, but he created a large hand made from his aura and slapped the creature and sent it flying several feet away.

Instead of it hitting the floor of the tower it melted into the ground and like a zooming shadow it moved along the ground and popped out behind Frey. Before Frey could react, the creature was on him, and it bit down hard on his arm.

Frey cried out and his staff fell to the ground. I rushed forward and grabbed the staff. I lifted the staff and swung it at the hell hound, but the staff was heavier than it looked and as the edge of the staff reached its fur the hell hound shifted back into shadow, and it melted into the ground.

Hua quickly wrapped a bandage onto Frey's arm covering the massive bite wound on his forearm and drawing moans from Frey.

Freya looked our way, worry heavy in her eyes, and tried to reach us, but the other hell hound was keeping her and Micah pinned.

We had four people on this hell hound and two on the other one. I attempted to make my way over to help them and even the odds, but the larger shadow beast emerged from the ground in front of me halting my progress.

The creature surprised me, and it would have bit into my arm like it had done Frey, but I was able to manifest my Faith and use it to protect the targeted area.

The fangs of the shadow beast bounced off of the construct, but the aura construct shattered from the force of the bite.

Before the creature could change back into shadow and retreat, I quickly brought the staff down on the beast.

I aimed for the eyes of the creatures, hoping to maim it instead of killing it but I missed, and the staff landed in between the shoulder and the neck.

The area where the staff had hit the hell hound glowed red and gave off a burning smell. The creature howled in pain and the other hell hound disengaged from the others and appeared at the side of its wounded partner.

Regret grabbed my heart, but I did not hesitate. I pulled the staff left hard, hoping to swipe both hell hounds at once.

The wounded hell hound took the time to melt into shadows, but its partner remained. The smaller hell hound took the blow from the staff with a yelp, yet it did not budge.

Its eyes seemed to only burn harsher with hate as a glowing red mark appeared on the right side of its face and it growled menacingly.

Before I could lift the staff again for another attack the smaller hell hound grabbed the staff with its jaws, pulling it out of my grip, and immediately bit down on my right hand.

I yelped in pain and watched as the staff vanished into a circle of shadow on the tower floor and as the staff vanished the other hell hound emerged.

It lunged onto me and slammed its paws onto my chest. At the same time pain erupted from my right hand.

I felt where my pinky and ring fingers used to be. It was numb at first and despite the hell hound on my chest I lifted my right hand and looked at what remained of it.

There was little blood and as I stared the numb sensation vanished. It was replaced by a warm feeling of pain that then elevated to a screaming hot pain.

I tried to scream but I only managed a croak and the pain in my body only intensified as the hell hound began to dig its claws into my abdomen.

I attempted to push the monster off, but I could not focus. My vision was blurry, and the pain was so much that it was all I could do to not pass out.

Odessa!

I cried her name in my head and out loud I thought, but she did not appear next to me, and she did not reply.

I saw Micah and Savant appear at my side. The hell hound on my chest ignored them and continued to claw into me. I felt the wetness on my stomach spread matching the tendrils of pain that traveled throughout my body.

My vision began to fade but before it went black, I saw Savant form a square aura construct and slam it down with his arm.

The square of aura sliced through the air like a guillotine, and it cut through the neck of the hell hound while it was in its physical form.

I was afraid it would cut through me too as it flew towards me but just before it would have cut into my chest the bordeaux aura dispersed.

The defeat of the smaller hell hound allowed me to stay conscious for a bit longer. I strained to move my head and I saw the bigger hell hound surrounded by Hua Frey and Freya.

"Micah!" Savant yelled.

Micah knelt at my side and immediately began to heal me. Their green aura was weak, and they ignored my fingers and focused on the damage to my abdomen.

"Give her this if you need to and try to find her fingers," Savant said, and he tossed them something that was wrapped in a dark black leaf.

"But the Court—" Micah started but Savant had turned to assist the others.

Micah looked at the thing in their hand and saw me looking and they smiled at me reassuringly.

"Don't worry," they said. "You're not going to die on my watch."

Their words made me feel butterflies in my stomach and I felt slightly better hearing their words.

Or perhaps it was just the blood loss getting to me.

"You're not pregnant, are you?" they asked.

"Definitely not," I managed, and Micah nodded their head.

They quickly unwrapped the parcel and broke what looked like bread in half. They then put half of the bread into my mouth.

The taste was just like the holy crisps that the Church of Eloah served on holiday. They were sweet like cream and crunchy.

Although Tripa Fons had given me the recipe and taught me how to make the secret holy crisps somehow this tasted just like them.

They were my favorite, and my mother knew that. She had done several deeds to be eligible to learn the recipe just so that she could make it for me at home, so we did not have to wait for the church to serve it.

As I swallowed the bread my fatigue abated some. My vision refocused and the ringing in my ears faded. It no longer felt like I was going to faint.

"Micah," I managed, and they smiled even wider at me.

"I got you, Arabella, I'm right here. Why don't you say a prayer to your God?" Micah said through clenched teeth.

I could feel the skin on my stomach slowly stitching itself under Micah's hands and it generated an intense itching sensation.

I resisted the urge to touch it and looked over at the other hell hound. It looked like the fight with it was winding down. The hound was dripping dark blood while the rest of the party had not gained any more injuries.

They pressured it towards the wall and the hell hound let out a mournful howl. It then sunk into the shadows and emerged just behind Savant, but Hua lifted her partitioned quarterstaff and slammed it onto the hell hound's head.

The hell hound whimpered, and Savant attempted the aura guillotine maneuver once more, but the hell hound managed to dodge, stumbling back, and avoiding the construct completely.

Savant rolled to the right and Hua followed behind him with her staff and caught the hell hound under the jaw.

The hell hound was thrust onto its side and Freya followed up with a dagger. She lunged onto the large hound and stabbed her dagger downwards.

The hell hound let out a sad whimper like a puppy, turned its head to the body of the other hell hound, and then it moved no more.

"Can any of you heal?" Savant asked.

Freya and Frey shook their heads in unison, but Hua hesitated.

She glanced at me, bleeding out on the floor of the tower and then she shook her head.

"I can heal a bit, but I've already been exhausted enough. I'll need every bit of magic I have left to defeat my father. I'm sorry, Arabella. Won't your god save you?"

Chapter EIGHT

savant

Her words were like a dagger in the back.

Although I knew the betrayal shouldn't have hit me so hard; after all, I had only met her mere hours before but her leaving me to bleed out felt as if she had made the wound herself.

Odessa would never. But then again Hua was not Odessa. She was nothing more than a stranger. What did she owe me?

I touched my stomach tenderly with the tips of what was left of my hands. Micah's healing had helped some, but I was still bleeding. I gripped my wrist and stared at my damaged hand in shock.

"My fingers," I whimpered. "Eloah, why?"

I watched as Hua looked at me bleeding on the tower floor. She stared at me, and I stared at her. She took a step towards me but then she frowned at me and gritted her teeth.

She grabbed Frey's wrist and pulled him up the stairs. They vanished without another glance. Freya looked at me for a moment.

"If I or my brother could heal, we would help," she said and then followed her brother and Hua onto the next floor.

"Here, try and stay still," Micah said.

With Savant's help Micah lightly coated my abdomen with bandages. I winced at the contact and exhaled deeply forcing myself not to panic.

A groan of pain escaped my lips as they tightened the bandages and then turned their focus onto my damaged hand.

I felt the pain in my abdomen still, but it was dull compared to the pain emanating from my palm. My right hand oozed, and I opened and closed my remaining fingers slowly.

"It looks worse than it is," Micah said studying the hand. "We can't regenerate lost limbs or fingers but if we can find the fingers, we can reattach them."

My heart dropped as Micah began to look once more for my fingers. Savant checked the area for more hell hounds and other enemies and determined that we were not in any more danger.

He sighed deeply and inspected the room with his eyes and then joined Micah in the scavenger hunt for my two fingers.

The sweet bread I had received from Micah had revitalized me, but it had not dulled the pain in my abdomen and hand. I felt wide awake, but the Mystio insisted I rest on my back while they searched.

I could read the expressions of the Mystio as they approached me. They had not found my fingers, that much was obvious, and it seemed I would be forever maimed this way.

"No luck," Savant said finally. "But one of the magicians in Jemny may be able to help us once all this is over with."

His words were unconvincing to me. Micah had just said that the fingers could not be restored and Jemny, the capital city of Damasyr, was weeks, if not months away.

Cool tears began to well in my eyes and flood down my cheeks. I wiped at them frantically, but they continued to slide.

I knew Savant and Micah were waiting for me so after a deep breath and a prayer of strength I gritted my teeth and sat up.

The First Constellation had taken enough from me. I would not let them take any more; from me or anyone else.

Samson.

Olympia.

Hong Tao.

Jesuit.

I made a list of their names in my mind and steadied myself onto one knee. It was time for payback. I forced myself to stand up straight and almost fainted immediately.

"I will be still for I know you are with me," I whimpered but the words did not carry the weight they usually did.

How could Eloah have allowed this to happen?

How could he have allowed Opulake to be destroyed?

How could he have allowed all of the other Opulakis to die?

What sort of god was that?

Micah had bandaged my hand as best as they could, but it continued to throb heavily, and it was clear I could not hold a weapon in my right hand any longer.

I would instead have to learn to fight with my left hand and until then I would be even more useless in a fight.

I felt full of magic thanks to the bread Micah had given me but because of my inadequacy with magic it was not much to rely on.

I had increased my skill greatly, but I was still a novice. Thanks to the hell hound, magic and my less dominant left hand were all I would have to defend myself in our next fight.

I shivered at the thought of fighting Hong Tao in a state that was even weaker than I had been the first time we had fought. On the beach I at least had all my fingers.

Savant and Micah gave me looks of concern, but they did not stop me as I made my way very slowly to the stairs that led to the next floor.

I used my Faith, and I was able to numb my wounds slightly so that I could ignore the pain signals my body was broadcasting but it would only last while I had magic, and while the spell was cast it would constantly drain on my magic reserves.

"Okay, I am ready," I said, feigning confidence and reassurance.

Savant nodded.

"Okay, I'll lead and Micah you take up the rear. Keep your guard up, the First Constellation leaders may be up here or worse."

As he finished speaking Savant turned and climbed the stairs after Hua and the twins without waiting for an answer.

I took a deep breath, glanced back at Micah, who nodded their head encouragingly and then I followed Savant up the tower stairs.

"This floor is clear," Savant called from above and as I entered the next floor, I saw that we were in a room of science.

There were several tables and shelves decorated with various glass containers and metal devices. I approached the first table and saw beakers that were filled with a lavender colored liquid.

Red, blue, and purple gemstones littered the tables, and I wondered what their purpose was. Rubies, sapphires, and amethysts had no common theme and were not often combined in jewelry and décor.

At the fall side of the tower was a wall of shelves that were filled with rings of black metal with large opals at their centers.

They seemed to radiate power and I felt drawn to them. They tugged at my mind as if they were alive and I took a half step forward and pointed at the rings with my good hand.

"Are these—"

"—*Imperi*," Micah finished.

Micah quickly reached out to grab one of the *imperi* before I could, but Savant caught their wrist and held it tightly.

"Wait, let's not be rash. This doesn't make sense. Think about it. If these really are *imperi* then where are the First Constellation and the others?" Savant asked.

Micah shrugged.

"Maybe they took one and left? The *imperi* were used for teleportation, right?" Micah replied. "My dwarven history isn't the best but these could be our way home."

I agreed with Micah's statement, but Savant shook his head. It made sense to me. It would also explain why the First Constellation was gone. They had found the *imperi* and were long gone by now. We were too late.

"No, look," he said, gesturing to the shelves. "Each shelf is filled to the brim with *imperi*. If someone had taken one there would be an empty spot on the shelves but there isn't."

He was right as far as I could tell. *Imperi* neatly lined each shelf, and it did not appear that any of the *imperi* were missing.

I groaned in confusion. Was this some kind of test or riddle? I wish the tower were more straight forward.

Typically, I did not mind philosophy and taking things slow, but I was mentally exhausted, and I wanted to rest and cry before going after the First Constellation or Odessa.

"So, what are you thinking," I asked. I gestured to the tower windows and to the city far below us. "This could be the highest floor of the tower. It's possible there isn't anything left for us."

"I hear you, Arabella, but there's something about this that doesn't feel right," Savant said. "We shouldn't be hasty."

He looked out the window of the tower at the cityscape below us.

"We don't have time to waste," I said in frustration.

"Give Lancer Solace a second, Arabella," Micah said with a smile.

Of course, they could smile. Their home had not been destroyed by the First Constellation. Their parents were still alive. And they still had all their fingers.

There was a whisper in my head. At first, I thought it was Odessa's voice in my mind, but it was not the raging whirlwind I had felt when I spoke to her through our empathy link.

power. you want power.

I turned around and faced the *imperi* once more. It could make me stronger. I glanced at Savant, and he was holding up two fingers and pointing at the city below us as he spoke with Micah.

I thought back to what Lady Gorin had said about me looking for power. I had denied it then but now I came to the conclusion that she had been right. How had she known what I had not yet recognized about myself?

I no longer wanted to be dead weight. I did not want to be saved over and over again. I wanted to be the savior. I just needed power to do so.

i can give you what you seek.

I reached for an *imperi* in front of me and grazed my finger against the black band. The metal felt as cold as ice and as hot as fire.

I picked up the *imperi* and heard a click behind me. Touching the ring sent my nerves into overdrive as they buzzed and itched.

I put the *imperi* on and waited for the power of the ring to flow into me. I blinked and the gem of the *imperi* glimmered, and I saw my missing fingers restored.

Their appearance caused me to gasp, and I involuntarily took a step away from the wall of *imperi*. As my foot landed, I felt water at my feet and suddenly I heard the roar of water. I glanced behind me and saw a current of water streaming into the room.

I gasped and looked back at the shelves of *imperi* once more but saw nothing but rings of bronze. Even the one on my finger was nothing more than a rusty ring.

It appeared to have been some sort of an illusion. I felt tears brew as I saw my fingers were still gone and I slipped off the fake *imperi* quickly and let it fall into the water.

The windows creaked and I saw that the view outside had changed and realized that we were lower than it seemed we had been. The windows slammed shut as sheets of metal sealed us in.

I turned and ran to Micah and Savant who were working to slow the water. Savant used his aura to block the tunnel the water was coming out of and was speaking to Micah quickly as I approached.

"Quick!" Savant said. "Look for a trigger or something to disable the water!"

I looked around frantically. I ran to the closest wall and ran my hands along it looking for a switch or recess on the wall.

What had I done?

Micah rushed past me saying words in a language I did not recognize. They glanced at Savant who was struggling to hold back the river of water with his aura.

Keeping the water back was probably a very heavy feat and the constant pressure I knew would be wearing Savant down.

Several minutes passed and we had yet to find a method to stop the water flow and Savant was beginning to sweat from the effort.

"Come on, guys," Savant said through gritted teeth. "I can't hold this much longer! There's got to be a trigger here somewhere! Look for a switch or something!"

Micah began to shout phrases in the incoherent dialect, and I watched as their golden brown eyes began to glow white and white mist like snow began to cloud around their body.

They then pointed their palms at the area where the water was pouring out and I watched in astonishment as the water slowed and froze, leaving an arc of ice from the hole to the tower floor.

Once the water had ceased its flow Micah let their palms fall to their side and then fell in a heap in the water.

Savant let his aura construct fade away and leaned against the temple wall. He lifted his arms above his head but took only a moment of rest before he made his way over to Micah's side.

The ice let out a thunderous *crack* and a large chunk of the ice slid down in a jagged arc and crashed into the floor of the tower.

As it slammed into the floor the ice shattered and spread out as a white cloud of frost but luckily the hole the water had been flooding out of remained frozen.

I joined Savant at Micah's side and would have knelt, but my gut protested so much I was forced to stand. I dared not speak or touch Micah. I had made a mistake so it was my fault they had fainted.

I had been tempted and given into that temptation and now Micah, someone I cared about, was laying in icy freezing water unconscious.

"They're okay," Savant said. "They just need a moment."

I nodded my head although I could not bring myself to meet his eyes.

While Micah rested, Savant began to run his hands along the walls.

"Why did you not have them do that in the first place?" I asked Savant in reference to Micah freezing the water.

"I did not want to expose their business," Savant replied, still studying the walls and floor. "Micah's powers are best kept secret, but I suppose they trust you."

"Look here, in case we run into a similar trap," Savant said, and before I could ask him more about Micah he outstretched his hand and touched a small square with the image of a large goat on it located on one of the walls I had already searched.

It was a dark purple tile on the floor of the tower near where Micah had collapsed. I had not seen it and neither had Micah, yet Savant had found it so easily.

As I quickly cleaned my glasses Savant pressed on the square lightly and even below the water, I heard a click as the room began to shake.

Behind Savant the wall where the fake *imperi* had been slid to the left and revealed a set of stairs that led upwards. The windows which had closed opened and revealed the city below once more.

I sighed in frustration. We were not as high up as it had previously appeared and there was no way someone could have found the trigger once the water had begun to pour into the room.

It was a death trap not a test.

Micah stirred and together Savant and I lifted them onto their feet. They wobbled as if they were dizzy but after a moment, they placed a hand on our opposite shoulders and stood up straight.

"Sorry," Micah said leaning their head forward. "You didn't have to wait for me. I would have caught up."

Savant slapped his hand onto Micah's shoulder and gripped it.

"My left hand, I could not do this without you," Savant said with a smile.

Micah smiled back at Savant and looked towards the staircase.

"Let's go, Lancer," they said and together we made our way towards the staircase. "*Ase Vertan.*"

"What does that mean?" I asked. "Is that the language you were speaking before?"

"*Ase Vertan,*" Savant said. "It is the motto of the Mystio. It means "We Will Win.""

"And will we?" I asked.

Savant and Micah nodded their heads together.

"We will."

Chapter NINE

mystio

The third floor of the tower was incomprehensible.

As I entered the third floor it seemed that this level of the tower was vastly larger than the previous floors. It appeared to be more of a hall.

I spun around in a circle in awe as the tower floor stretched farther than it appeared any room could. When I had looked up at the tower of magic from outside, each floor had appeared to be the same size.

Savant slowly took a step forward. I followed cautiously and Micah came up the stairs behind me. They gasped at the sight of the third floor.

"This makes no sense," Micah said as they looked at how far the room stretched.

I was having trouble comprehending what I was seeing myself. Near the stairs was a black table that seemed to hum with energy and on it was a large purple bowl full of heart shaped fruit.

I wanted to grab one and inspect it but after my incident with the *imperi* I decided to refrain from touching anything.

"I bet you're wishing Adonis and I were on opposite missions now," Micah said with a smile and to my surprise Savant laughed and nodded his head.

I wondered how the Mystio Adonis knew so much more about the dwarves than the other Mystio. I had assumed that they would have all gotten the same training.

"It must be another illusion," Savant said becoming serious once more. "Be careful. We don't want to trigger another trap."

He did not look at me or say my name, but I got his meaning and had the nerve to blush. I had messed up I knew, and I tried to shake thoughts of the *imperi* from my head.

My eyes wandered to the bowl of fruit once more. I knew the heart shaped fruit had to have been there for years, yet the fruit shone as if they were freshly picked from their branches or vines just this morning. They were the color of grapes and only four remained in the bowl.

"Do you think the fruit here is safe?" I asked Savant and I was not surprised when he shook his head as his answer.

I licked my lips in hunger. I was starving. I could not even say how long it had been since I had last eaten. My sense of shame from the previous floor outweighed my hunger and I pulled my eyes off of the fruit and followed Savant.

We slowly began to proceed farther into the room. The walls were made of the same material as the tower itself but were devoid of any decorations and designs.

Before each step forward Savant inspected where each foot would land as to avoid triggering any traps and he kept his hands outstretched to make sure nothing was in front of him that was outside his perception.

I mimicked his foot placements and tried to remain patient. We were moving so slowly and there was no sign of other stairs at the other end of the room or any signs of those who had come up before us.

Eventually we made it to the opposite wall, and I saw a bowl on a small pedestal. I thought it might be more of the fruit, but the bowl was empty and underneath carved in the pedestal read: *"Only Those With Fire In Their Blood May Enter"*.

"Fire in their blood," Micah said. "What do you think that means?"

"Dwarves," Savant said. "Their magic can conjure fire. They are those with fire in their blood."

"Only those with fire in their blood may enter," I repeated.

What could that mean? Were we unable to proceed if we did not have a dwarf with us? If that was the case where had the others gone?

There had to be another answer and my mind thought of Lady Gorin. I wish I knew of a way to find the dwarf or that I had convinced her to come with us.

"I do not suppose either of you know any dwarves?" I asked.

I knew that the dwarves had long vanished from the kingdom of Damasyr. I had heard that some had gone east to Tyvent, and I thought back to when my mother had said she would bring me back a dwarven trinket if she did meet a dwarf while in Tyvent.

Savant and Micah glanced at each other, but I couldn't read their expressions.

"Perhaps we can make a fire," Micah suggested. "I have my sticks."

"It's worth a shot," Savant said.

Micah reached into their pocket and pulled out two black sticks of metal. On one of the grips was a small compass and on the other it appeared that there was a small whistle.

"What is that?" I asked.

"Mag Sticks," Micah replied. "Short for Magnesium Sticks. They make it easy to start fires when we need them. Left has a compass, right has an emergency whistle, but the horses hate the whistle."

Micah scraped the black sticks together over the bowl and I watched in silent awe as sparks of flame burst forth from the contact and fell into the bowl.

Micah continued scraping to create more sparks and the more that filled the bowl the more the bowl began to glow. As it glowed the purple on the bowl shifted into gold as the tower itself had.

After a minute of scraping their Mag Sticks Savant pulled out his own Mag Sticks and began to contribute to the bowl on the pedestal.

"Keep an eye out while we try this," Savant recommended, and I nodded.

I glanced around us, but we were still alone on the third floor of the tower. I wondered once more where the others had gone.

Eventually there were enough flames to fill the bowl and the bowl was completely gold. The Mystio halted their scraping and I waited for something to happen, but the only change was that the flames died and the bowl returned to its normal purple hue.

"It did not work," I said disappointed.

"Considering everything else we've been through, that did seem a bit easy," Micah admitted but they did not smile.

At their words the pedestal began to hum and the three of us retreated. The pedestal sunk into the floor of the tower and where it had stood a hole began to expand until it was large enough for a person to fit through it, yet it continued to grow.

I looked into the hole but saw not the floor below us but a world of flames. I saw a red sky and rivers of molten rock. In the distance there were many volcanoes with dark smoke billowing out of them.

Suddenly a large snake like creature emerged from the hole. As it cleared the portal the hole closed behind it leaving the world of flames behind.

The snake's center was a grey black with white lines that glowed slightly and ran around the snake's body. It stood two men high, and altogether was as long as four men.

Large white bristles hung loosely at its side until they flared up across the snake's entire length and began to drip a yellow liquid. Its eyes were large and were the same color as the lava I'd seen.

The snake's maw was blood red and a long orange forked tongue stretched out past its black fangs. It hissed at us, and its black spittle landed on the tower floor causing smoke to rise.

"Watch out for its venom," Savant said.

"Can't we catch a break?" Micah said as they quickly armed themselves with a throwing knife in each of their hands.

"What is it?" I asked.

"I don't know," Savant said. "It's not in our bestiary."

Great, I thought.

The snake without warning lunged forward toward me with its jaw open wide. I do not know why it chose me, perhaps because I was the fat one, perhaps with my injuries or even without my injuries I appeared the weakest.

I froze for a second before panic took over and I threw myself onto the tower floor, but I still felt the tremendous heat above me as the snake passed inches abov me.

Micah yelled to get the snake's attention and once it faced them Micah aimed two throwing knives at the snake's eyes.

Both knives hit their mark but as they sunk into the snake's pupils they melted and were absorbed into the snake's eyes.

"Okay Plan B," Micah said, and using their ice magic created a dark blue sword of ice. They exhaled deeply and a large white cloud billowed out from between their lips.

Micah exhaled once more and created a second ice sword and handed it to Savant. Savant could not hold it with his bare hand as Micah could, so he gripped the sword with his shirt sleeve as a buffer for his skin.

I heard the fire snake nearby so I tore my eyes away from Micah, picked myself up, and rolled away as far as I could from the monster.

I wanted a cool sword made of ice too, but I was not very good with sword and Micah look very unsteady from the creation of the ice constructs so I did not speak up.

The fire snake's skin glistened and looked smooth. I figured it would be weak to slashes but it was so hot it seemed impossible to even get close enough to slash it.

Savant quickly cloaked himself in his purplish-red aura and moved in quickly towards the snake. With a flourish he twisted the ice blade to catch the snake's attention.

Once the snake's eyes caught the glint of the sword Savant outstretched his left hand and created a large hand made out of aura and slammed it into the snake's jaw.

The blow lifted the snake into the air and its head slammed onto the temple's floor. Savant dispersed his aura and gasped. His hand was blotchy and beginning to blister.

"It burns even through my aura, be careful," he said and then cursed as his right hand began to swell like a severe allergic reaction.

"That hurts a lot," he admitted as he was forced to transfer his ice sword to his left hand to wield it better.

While the snake was recovering, I rushed forward, and with my Faith I imagined a sword like Micah had but I was only able to construct something more like a long dagger. Swallowing my disappointment, I stabbed downwards into the snake's tail as hard as I could.

The dagger pierced into the snake and then shattered causing the snake to lift its head in pain bringing a smile to my face.

It was a small victory and in response the snake billowed and opened its mouth wide and sent a wave of hot air towards us. I could see the heat haze created by its breath and knew it would be deadly if it hit us.

Savant started his aura, but it appeared his injury delayed his construct or perhaps he was tired from his previous use of magic because only sparks of bordeaux leapt from his fingers.

Micah managed to throw up their green aura instead and created a crooked box that prevented most of the heat from reaching us, but it was still hot enough to cause my body to sweat profusely.

The breath blazed over us for almost a whole minute and when it finally abated Micah let their aura fade and they fell onto one knee.

The snake also seemed tired from the effort. Its skin was slightly duller and gave off less heat.

I wanted to take advantage of this, so I ran towards it and managed to create a short sword with my Faith and instead of stabbing I slashed down on the snake's tail.

About two feet of the snake's tail was severed and as the skin parted steam scalded my face and its blood quickly began to burn my feet.

I yelped and jumped away but not before the bottom of both my feet were burnt. Being barefoot did not bother me as most Opulakis went barefoot excluding certain seasons and ceremonies but the burn made each foot uncomfortable to stand on.

The snake rose as high as it could and the bristles on the its skin grew stiff and quicker than I could react several shot out.

I manifested my Faith, but I was too slow, and the construct was too fragile, and two bristles pierced me: one in the shoulder and one in the abdomen.

I cried out and fell onto my knees. I knew better than to just remove them but where they pierced me I could feel my body going numb as if it was turning off my cells one by one.

I looked towards Savant and Micah and saw that both of them had repelled the snake's bristles, but they were still recovering from the attack.

The snake looked at me and I could tell I was its target, but my body had become numb, and I could no longer move.

"M—" I tried to say but my tongue was numb, and it prevented me from speaking.

The snake slid towards me, and I felt its lip grip me and felt its fang dig into my other shoulder. I let out a motionless and silent cry and all I could see was the ceiling of the tower before I slid into an inferno of darkness.

Chapter TEN

eloah

Inside of the fire snake I was being burned alive.

The heat inside prevented me from breathing properly and I was still unable to move my body. The lining of the snake's throat was slick with a liquid that dripped onto my skin and seared into it.

If I could gain control of my limbs perhaps, I could climb up the snake's throat but they refused to obey me, and I remained frozen in place.

If I could manifest my Faith, I could send it forward into the dark to reach for the snake's uvula and cause it to throw me up, assuming snakes had uvulas.

The constant pain made it hard to focus. I tried to bring my Faith out several times but each time it was only a brief lighting of neon before fading away.

It was hopeless.

I could feel my skin sizzling away, but it no longer hurt as it had before. It was almost a pleasant experience, and I began to feel a warm and happy feeling in my chest.

I smiled and let my body relax and I waited for the darkness to claim me completely. Besides, what did I have waiting for me in the light?

My parents were dead. They would not be returning to Damasyr. If they were alive they would not have left me here alone for so long.

My mentor, Tripa Fons was also dead. He had been killed by Samson but at the thought of Samson, I remembered my vow to kill all of the remaining First Constellation leaders.

It caused me to stir in discomfort. I had made a vow and they were quite serious, but I could not help that I had been eaten and was being dissolved by a giant fire snake!

It seemed pointless now. The world was full of evil people and if I did kill the leaders, new ones would appear to take their place. I did not want to spend the rest of my life fighting, especially against the same organization in a lifelong blood feud.

No, I decided it would be easier to give up here and save myself from the storm of pain and stress that would come with living longer.

My best friend Estella was dead. No one would ever know me like she did, not even Odessa. Estella and I had gone through the same Elohan upbringing, and both our parents had vanished to Tyvent. No one else could relate to the void that their absence had left in my chest.

My betrothed Skylark was dead along with the rest of the men of Opulake. Any possibility of me raising my social status was gone. It would be impossible for me to attain an elevating marriage in a different settlement.

I did not care about social status, so I was not sure why I was even thinking about it at that moment. I thought it was because status was the only thing I would have gained in a marriage with Skylark.

I would see them all again soon. I wished for nothing else more. As Faithful Children of Eloah we could look forward to an afterlife in the Mountains of Umi

In the Mountains of Umi we would be surrounded by our friends and family, those that had died at least. Along with them we would be allowed to feast and play games until the Return occurred.

I closed my eyes, but thoughts of Odessa infiltrated my mind. I squirmed and found I could move now slightly.

I slowly reached out blindly but the snake was moving now and as it did its inside shook and soon my stomach was upset. I forced myself to focus and regain my course of thought.

I had been thinking of Odessa and at the thought of her, I remembered why I could not die. If I died Odessa probably would too. Even if I did not have anything left to live for, she had plenty.

I hoped she was making good progress on her journey home. I wished I could have reached her with our empathy link. I wished for a lot of things.

Odessa had her sister, Talicia, and her father Grimke. Her home Pavrenes still stood and even right now she was working hard to protect it. Did I have the right to rob them of her?

I opened my eyes even though I was still left in darkness. I owed Odessa enough to at least die fighting.

Ignoring the pain, I manifested and cloaked my body in my Faith. Even though my skin was still irritated from the burning it felt slightly better.

"Okay," I said to myself, trying to come up with a plan but it sounded more like "bloblay" with my swollen tongue.

Unfortunately, I still could not move my body very much. I could still manipulate my Faith without moving but it was harder. I grew frustrated and my Faith faded leaving me in darkness once again.

I let out a fragment of a yell and thought about how I hated the sound of it. I sounded like a wounded animal.

"I will be still for I know you are with me," I whispered as tears continued to roll down my cheeks.

I could do nothing else, so I prayed to Eloah for a miracle. He rarely intervened in our world, but we had recorded four miracles throughout our history where he had.

The First Miracle was when Eloah had saved the First Prophet Rutabaga Zaebos from the legendary Dark Ranger Vasenya Longsword. If he had lost his confrontation with her, the Elohan Church of Dresden would not have been established.

The Second Miracle was when Eloah had saved half of Dresden, the capital city at the time, from the Great Flood. The northern half of Dresden would become North Dresden, the main hub of Elohan culture.

I wondered now if the Great Flood was the same that had covered the dwarven city of Jormondor. Eloah had spared most of Dresden, but the dwarves had managed to save all of Jormondor with their magic and technology.

The Third Miracle was one of secrecy. Tripa Fons had known what it was, but he had never told me. I was sure it was just as important as the other Miracles though.

The Fourth Miracle was during the Rebellion of the New Crowns. When the previous dynasty had been overthrown about fifty years ago the new king had wanted to destroy the Church of Eloah but the Forty-Fourth Prophet, Pensilea, would end up being engaged to the king and by her marriage the extermination of the Church of Eloah had been averted.

Was I worth a fifth miracle? I could never be as great as Rutabaga Zaebos, Tripa Fons, or Pensilea Zhang. I was only Arabella of Opulake.

Eloah. Please, I need your help. Please, do not forsake me.

I said the words in my head hoping to feel his Blessing. Eloah had the power to move me to safety or he could just destroy the snake. He could empower the Mystio to help them save me.

But none of that happened. I knew I could not lose Faith. If I did not believe, I would not be able to use my magic anymore.

"Eloah!" I yelled.

Liquid from inside the snake dripped into my mouth, burning my tongue, and causing it to swell to the point where I could not move it in my mouth and was forced to breathe through my nose.

The air stung my nostrils as I inhaled. It was too much. I could not bear it any longer. I decided to embrace the numbing effect satisfied that I had fought as hard as I could.

I blinked but as my eyes shut instead of seeing blackness I was immersed in green light. I blinked hard thinking I was hallucinating now and when I opened my eyes I was elsewhere.

I was underground somewhere but it seemed I was no longer in Jormondor, although the architecture appeared to be similar.

The cavern was lined with glowing emeralds that shone their brilliant light on us leaving everything in a shade of green.

"Ah, Arabella," a deep voice said and the wall next to me shifted.

I found I was able to move, and I took a step back as I realized the wall was actually part of a large man's leg.

I craned my neck as I saw a man who stood about thirty feet high. He wore no shoes revealing very hairy feet with large toes that were shiny and trimmed.

He wore brilliant turquoise pants under an orange long sleeved tunic. On his head over his long, thick black hair was a brimless cap that matched his tunic.

On his back was a bow made of red wood wrapped in green fabric that had to be at least twenty feet long with an empty quiver next to it.

His eyes were green too like the emerald that shone from the ceiling almost as if his irises were made of gemstones themselves.

I was speechless for a moment. I had never seen a man or bow so tall. I knew that I was in the presence of something greater than myself.

I remained speechless until I realized that my tongue was no longer swollen and that I could speak once more. In fact, I felt none of the pain I had before I had appeared here.

"Who are you?" I asked in wonder.

"**Huh**?" the man grumbled. "**Speak up.**"

The planet itself seemed to shake as the man sat down, crossed his legs, and leaned forward toward me. He towered over me, and his shadow left me in a weak darkness.

I swallowed hard and wet my lips with my tongue.

"Who are you?" I repeated.

"**I have been called many names and titles, but you would know me as Eloah**," he thundered.

"Eloah," I whispered and immediately bowed low on my knees.

"I have chosen you as my next prophet," he said and the disconnect I was experiencing increased into full on shock. **"I will communicate my will to you, and you will lead and protect my people."**

"Your next prophet," I whispered. "I can not. I am not strong enough."

"I do not choose my prophets based off of strength as you would define it," Eloah said. **"And I have not made a mistake as you would suggest next."**

"You must have made a mistake," I said before I registered what he had said.

Eloah smiled at me and when his lips parted I saw that he had sharp teeth like I had never seen in a human or an animal.

"You will be my Prophet, conduit to my will and in return I shall grant you my Blessing. Do you accept, Arabella of Opulake?"

"Yes," I said without hesitation. Access to the Blessing of Eloah was my father's lifetime achievement. I knew he would be proud that I had been chosen.

Eloah nodded but I felt no different.

"Is The Return approaching?" I asked.

"We are at your limit now it seems. I must send you back," Eloah said. **"You have my Blessing; avenge those you have lost."**

His eyes began to glow bright green and then burst into green flames. A ball of the flames emerged and soared towards me.

As it approached, I could feel its heat, but I forced myself not to flinch. The fire sunk into my chest and although it did not hurt like real fire it was extremely uncomfortable.

"You will not be able to contain my Blessing for long. There is no time to waste, but you should have enough to heal your fingers. Now go, my Prophet."

I saw my form becoming transparent and I realized I was beginning to fade away. I waved my hands through the air at Eloah hoping to catch his attention and halt him.

"Wait!" I shouted. "Lord Eloah, are my parents still alive?"

o

I opened my eyes and found that I was back in the snake once more. The pain returned stronger than ever, but it lasted only a second.

The red in my hair began to glow as if it had caught fire and extended all the way up to my roots. My vision became clearer, and although I could see in the darkness, everything was shaded in greyness.

I was able to move my arms once more and saw that when I took my full moon glasses off I could actually see better without them, so I folded and pinned them to my shirt's neckline.

I pressed my lips together and hummed as I extended my arms with fingers open. I could feel a tingle in my right hand and saw the nub where my ring finger had been slowly growing back like a lizard regrowing its tail.

I balled my fists and thrust them open and as I did the inside of the snake began to quickly expand and after a moment of resistance, the snake's body burst leaving the tower floor covered in gore.

The ground around me was smoky and covered with the insides of the snake. Its head wriggled on the tower floor for a moment before becoming stationary and its eyes lost their life and turned grey.

My skin steamed and I could feel a heat inside me churning. I did not fall onto the ground and instead my feet hovered several feet off the ground.

I did a spin in the air and saw that I could now fly. The Elohan green dress I had worn before was gone and I was now in the official garb of the Prophet of Eloah.

I wore tight black pants with dark brown sandals that had a copper colored thong that ran between my big toe and the rest. I wore a chest piece similar to the kind the Mystio wore except it was dark green with a trim of copper at the bottom. Under the armor I wore a long sleeved black shirt.

The outfit was shaped perfectly for me, and I thought the coolest part was the scarf. The scarf was dark green, and it levitated around my shoulders.

I could feel the Blessing of Eloah. It felt like streams of lightning ran through my veins. I felt like I could do anything. I felt no trace of my injuries and saw more of my finger had returned.

I looked down at Micah and Savant. They were battered and bruised, and I knew they had tried their hardest to get me out of the snake.

Micah's face was one of amazement, but Savant looked at me suspiciously.

I scoffed. After all, what did his opinion matter now? I was the Prophet of Eloah and with Eloah's Blessing I was stronger than the both of them.

I was stronger than Odessa.

I was stronger than Samson.

I was stronger than anyone.

I looked at the bowl once more and then at the ceiling above us. I still did not know the answer to the bowl's riddle and did not have time to spare.

I raised my palm at the ceiling and felt a surge of power. A large square sized twenty feet across each way turned white and disintegrated and cloaked us in a layer of salt that burned at our eyes.

I glanced at the Mystio. Neither's uniform was pristine. They were both breathing heavily and burned all across their bodies. They could not match my shine, yet I owed them both a lot.

"Grab my hands," I instructed.

Micah did not hesitate, and they grabbed my left hand and gripped it, but Savant hesitated. He had reached his unswollen hand out but had not made contact with mine yet.

"How are you doing this?" he asked but I shook my head in frustration.

"Later, there is no time right now," I said quickly. "Do you want to catch the First Constellation or not?"

Savant gripped my right hand and nodded his head in response. I tightened my grip on both of them and I sent a wave of my magic into them.

Both Mystio groaned but after the glow subsided their wounds were completely healed. Even the swelling in Savant's hand was gone and despite the spell I felt no difference in my magic reserves.

I looked upwards and just by thinking about it my body responded. I soared upwards easily bringing the Mystio with me and soon we were on the next floor of the tower.

I saw a reflective room coated in what looked like mirrors. I saw myself with glowing green eyes like Eloah's and instead of red and black my hair was neon green like the color of my Faith was when I manifested it. My skin was lined with black glyphs of a language I could not read.

So, this is the Blessing of Eloah.

I did not focus on the mirrors for long and as we neared the next ceiling. I told it to dissolve and as it did we were drenched in water as the hole that appeared poured a mighty downpour of magic onto us.

The force was tremendous, and I expected I would falter yet I swam through the air and then soared through the water until I was above its surface.

I felt something pierce my skin and looked downwards to see my arms coated in bright red slugs. They bit into my flesh, and I could feel them sucking. I winced as Savant pinched one and it went limp before throwing it below us.

His own body was under assault by slugs and Micah's also. I halted our ascent for a moment. I focused on expelling the slugs and with a boom of sound the slugs were yanked from our bodies leaving dark blue rings on our skin for just a moment before I had the Blessing heal our sores.

Out of the water a large metal shark glided in a high arc towards us. Savant raised his arm but there was no need.

I quickly transferred Savant and Micah to my left arm so that they both were holding onto my forearm. With my right arm free I raised my arm, the water below rose in response, and I wrapped it around the shark.

The metal creature protested but it was in vain as I tightened the water around the shark, pulled it back into the water below, and threw it towards the tower floor.

I saw it hit the floor hard in a burst of sparks before it sunk into the hole in the ground I had created towards the previous floor.

I looked upwards and created another square for us to traverse through. I heard the sounds of fighting and looked toward the commotion and saw Hua along with the twins, Frey and Freya fighting against a hulking figure nearby.

It was light grey, neither male nor female, and dripped what looked like clay onto the obsidian floor. Its eyes burned like hot coals, and it had no nose or mouth on its face.

The creature pulled a large clump of its body off and sent it speeding toward Frey. Frey attempted to dodge it, but he was limping, and it appeared his leg was injured.

Hua raced towards him. She jumped onto him and pushed him onto the floor. He was saved by her from the clay creature's attack, but the clay caught Hua by her hand and dragged her through the air along with it.

The clay slammed into the wall with a loud slap and Hua's body followed quickly behind with her head banging against the tower wall.

She struggled there for a moment and then her eyes closed, and her head drooped. Her body continued to sway there momentarily, and the clay slid down some, but her body remained hanging there limply.

Frey called her name and raced towards her. Freya looked at Hua and Frey and then saw us hovering above them.

"Help us, please," she called.

I glanced at them, and I knew I should have helped them but the power surging in me demanded to be released as holy retribution. I hesitated.

"Arabella," Micah said.

They only said my name, one word, yet I understood what they were communicating.

They had abandoned me but that did not mean we should abandon them. We had to be better. I understood the message, but I felt something tug on me and I began to fly towards the next floor once more.

I paused once more as I felt Micah release my arm. They fell towards the ground into a roll and without hesitating they raced towards Hua, the twins, and the clay monster.

Savant looked me in the eyes and nodded but I did not know what it meant. He released my arm and then raced after Micah.

I shook my head. Was he not the one who had insisted we pursue the First Constellation? Traitors like them did not deserve my help. The Blessing of Eloah was reserved for me alone.

It seemed only I was strong enough to do what needed to be done.

"Fine," I said to no one. "I will do it alone."

Chapter ELEVEN

eufaula

I aimed my left hand at the ceiling above me and there was a loud splashing sound as a large hole appeared as an opening.

I closed my heart on Micah and the others. They had made their choice and had decided to side with Hua and the twins.

I was deigned to seek vengeance for my God; I could not disobey. I did not *want* to. The First Constellation deserved retribution.

If I did not avenge Estella, who would?

If I did not avenge Tripa Fons, who would?

If I did not avenge Eufaula, who would?

The list went on in my head. Hong Tao had decimated the Mystio on the beach and I had to take him and Olympia down now while I was imbued with the Blessing of Eloah.

I soared upwards and as I passed through the hole and entered the realm of the next floor I was immersed in a world of ice and snow.

I shivered against my will even though I did not really feel the cold. The Blessing of Eloah had grown warm to compensate for the extreme cold.

I knew it was a magic of some kind that brought about the cold for it made no sense for there to be this sort of climate in the tower.

Snow buffeted me as if I were in a blizzard and seemed to fall from the ceiling itself. I looked up and saw large dark grey clouds above me that the snow drifted down from.

I was not able to think about the clouds for long as I felt the wind suddenly curl around me like a snake constricting a rodent.

It reminded me of how I had grabbed the metal shark with the water, but it seemed it was the air itself that grappled with me.

As the living wind tightened even with the Blessing of Eloah cloaking my body, I began to feel the extreme cold pressing against my skin.

Arabella and the Tower of Magic

I did not do well in the cold. Opulake was a southern town and it had never snowed. I wish I could take more time to appreciate the snow, yet it was so cold that I could not imagine ever enjoying the chill.

My body let off a large cloud of steam as the wind lashed at my skin. I willed the wind to stop, and the breeze froze, causing the flakes of frosts to sparkle around me as brilliant specks of light blue.

At a closer inspection I saw what was assaulting me was not the wind sentient, but hundreds of small pale blue insects.

It was the insects that sparkled around me not snowflakes. Though they did not move I could see their icy blue wings locked in flight and their yellow eyes flittered left and right.

I grabbed for one and it felt like a cold beetle in between my fingers. It was so cold it burned through the heat of the Blessing. Bringing it closer I could see gears turning within its exoskeleton.

It was alive! Just as the shark, the dog, and the spiders had been made of metal these bugs were also manufactured. It was even more impressive because of how small they were. Whose fingers could work on such a small creature.

I wondered at all the kinds of magic the dwarves had implanted in their architecture and the creatures of earth and metal they had molded. Such things no longer existed unless they remained far to the north or west in the great cities of Damasyr like Almonaster and Ichor.

Having wasted enough time, I levitated and extended my arms out with my palms open and in a flash of light the bugs around me lost the light in their eyes and they fell like snowflakes towards the floor of the tower.

I rose towards the ceiling irritated and wondered how many floors of the tower there were and when I would catch up to Hong Tao and Olympia.

It had looked quite tall from the outside. I knew the Blessing of Eloah was not permanent and I did not want to be bothered with an obstacle on every floor.

Gratefully, when I rose to the next floor, I saw that it was bare and empty besides a bucket with an inscription underneath it on a golden plaque.

I was not close enough to read what it said, and I did not bother to investigate further. With the Blessing of Eloah, I could disregard the riddle and rise to the next floor without wasting time.

I rose higher and as I had done with the previous two floors I dissolved the ceiling once more and passed through it.

I enjoyed the thrill of the Blessing. After the use of it I did not feel fatigued by its use as I did when I used my Faith alone. It seemed my power was unlimited.

Arabella and the Tower of Magic

The moment I completely passed through the hole and flew onto the next floor the ground below me instantly repaired itself and I was sealed in a completely white room.

It was like the previous hall shaped room but this one was larger and longer, if that was believable. It seemed to stretch on endlessly, an infinite whiteness and the longer I stared the dizzier I became.

I inhaled only to find that there was no oxygen in the room, and I began to panic. Even with my Blessing it seemed I still needed to breathe.

My breathing became deep and fast as my lungs demanded air but there was none to be found. The room suddenly shifted as if it had been turned sideways.

The sudden shift disoriented me, and I lost my focus on my levitation and fell onto my knees. The room seemed to shift once more, and I had to force myself not to throw up as I was tossed onto my side.

Adding to my nausea I became lightheaded. My vision blurred and I tried to focus on what I needed to do but I could not find an equilibrium.

I aimed my hand at the ceiling and dissolved a square of it. I instinctively took a deep breath, but it was airless, yet I managed to rise to my feet.

I bent my knees and jumped towards the hole. I rose several feet into the air and the Blessing of Eloah caught me and I flew towards the hole.

As I neared it my lungs began to recover, and I gulped in the fresh air greedily. Reaching the hole, I saw that I had actually blasted a hole in the side of the tower and not the ceiling like I had planned.

I took several deep breaths, and my lungs were quickly restored to normal condition by the Blessing of Eloah. I exhaled deeply and began to rise but then I felt a familiar breeze roll into my mind.

Arabella?

It was Odessa! It was the first time she had reached out with our empathy link. I smiled, composed myself like normal, and responded.

Odessa. How is your journey going?

Not great. I managed to find my sword, Adonis had it, but things have been unbelievable since we left Pavrenes. Our first night we met a banshee, and it was Eufaula O'Connor. She—

I interrupted her at the sound of Eufaula's name.

Wait, you met Eufaula?

Yes, and she gave me a message. My boyfriend, Colden, is in trouble back home. The First Constellation has teamed up with a guild from Cypress. There was a girl. I tried to save her, but she died.

I was surprised so much had happened and realized more time had passed than I had expected.

Odessa had been through a lot when I had expected she would have had an easy return trip home.

Wow, are you okay? How far are you from Pavrenes?

I'm fine now. The Mystio have something called whey. It's like a bread, but it got me in top shape, and Adonis healed my hand. He says we should arrive at Pavrenes by tonight or tomorrow.

Despite Odessa's troubles she always remained focused on her goal. Nothing would stop her. Nothing *could* stop her. Like I had said, she was a hurricane.

I realized it must have been whey that Micah had given me before. It must be a treat that all Mystio kept in their inventory.

As she spoke, I could visualize her speaking. She often spoke with her hands and her hazel eyes always seemed to be shining.

You are so close. Stay smart. I will let Savant know what you have told me when I can. Let me know if you need anything, okay?

Odessa slowly flowed out of my mind, and I felt her presence waver as if she wanted to say more but she did not, and her spirit faded away.

I wondered what she would do in my position. Odessa revolved around her friends and family, but I wondered if she would still have been as unstoppable if she had lost everything as I had.

If she had no home, no family, no friends, no future, would she still be as driven?

That was my position. Except for the role of Prophet that Eloah had given me I had none of the things that drove Odessa. Vengeance was my only purpose now.

I knew the answer to my question concerning what Odessa would do but I did not want to dwell on it. The glow of my skin diminished for a moment, and I remembered why Eloah had given me his Blessing.

Revenge. Vengeance. Retribution.

I looked out the hole in the tower and studied the dwarven city of Jormondor. The city was dead and unmoving. There was nothing that remained here but monsters and ghosts, but there was also a great power here too.

If I could get my hands on the *imperi* I could gain that power. With that power I could be the next Prophet of Eloah properly. I could protect those who needed protection and defeat those who dared to inconvenience the Children of Eloah.

I looked over the city of Jormondor once more for the space I had met Lady Gorin in, but I did not see it. I did not expect to.

I did not even know how I had passed out in her presence and woke up in Hua's. The area was probably magical and hidden, perhaps even further underground.

I wished the dwarven woman had come. She would have known how to bypass the monsters and traps that plagued the tower of magic and saved us a lot of time.

I looked upwards and wondered. After a moment of hesitation, I jumped out from the hole and the Blessing of Eloah caught me once more.

I glanced downwards thinking about the welfare of Micah and the others, but it was only for a second before I was flying upwards towards the highest level of the tower.

I would deal with no more monsters, and no more traps, riddles, or extreme environments. I could bypass them with Eloah's help if Lady Gorin would not assist me. I did not need her either. After all, she was no god.

As I reached the top of the tower, I saw that the edges of the top were lined in brick squares like battlements.

There was no sign of the First Constellation, and I thought it was unlikely that I had beat them to the top after I had fallen unconscious more than once and how many obstacles I had encountered.

It was hard to know how much time had passed yet the tower continued to glow gold, so I believed that there was still time to stop whatever they had planned.

In the center of the highest tower floor was a square pyramid that seemed to glow as if it was under a purple light although none shone on it.

The pyramid was made out of more of the black metal. I floated towards it but retreated as there was a flash of light and suddenly beams of purple light reached towards me.

I felt the hair on my body raise as the rays reached me and I felt that if not for my Blessing I would have died from the contact.

Once they faded, I levitated in front of the pyramid and touched it. A flame of purple erupted at my contact and set my hand ablaze.

I could not feel the heat of the flames, but they quickly began to climb from my hand and up my arm. I cloaked my other hand with my Faith and wiped the flames off and they landed on the tower floor in a *hiss*.

I watched as the flames transitioned from fire and formed into a small purple goo that pulsed with bursts of lightning. It expanded and contracted quickly and began to rise until it was the height of a person.

It widened and at its base it split at the bottom until it formed something like legs and then towards the top arms split off too and a blob at the top formed into a head and a mouth appeared with a glowing purple light emanating from inside.

The purple ooze transitioned into brown, and by its curves it was clear that the blob was impersonating a woman.

The woman was naked for a moment, but the brown ooze dripped and shifted into an Elohan green dress that covered her body, yet her feet remained bare.

I gasped as I looked at the woman's face.

"Mother?" I asked but as the magical goo stopped evolving, I saw that it was not my mother although the facial features were similar.

The woman was me.

Chapter TWELVE

arabella

The Other Me looked at me and raised her fists. She did not possess the Blessing of Eloah as I did. Her lack of the Blessing exposed her as an inferior phony.

I could beat her.

Once again, I was in awe of the scale of the magic that the dwarves had employed in the tower. I had never even heard of a magic that could duplicate someone.

How could they have lost to humans when they yielded such technology and magic? I wondered.

The Other Me did not appear to be an illusion, unless she was a very good one. She took a deep breath, and I could see her breath as it made contact with the cold air and then she rushed towards me.

I watched her pull back her left hand and then swung her palm at me and immediately I could tell she was a better fighter than I. The Other Me moved with a quick gait, and she was light on her feet.

She came at me exuding a neon green aura like mine, yet it was thick and rose from her body in wisps. Her aura filled the air with the scent of sage.

The Other Me swung towards me and I managed to drop below her strike but before I could evade further the Other Me twisted and lifted her right hand.

Her aura flared out and cloaked her hand, and then she slapped me with a burst of magic that sent me flying backwards.

The impact did not hurt much but it disrupted my concentration, and I landed on the tower floor. I took a deep breath and tried to levitate once more.

The Other Me did not give me breathing room. She quickly closed the distance between us and swiped her right hand towards me.

I managed to lean back and dodge once more but when I attempted to kick her with my left leg, she leapt backwards and out of range before I could reach her.

Before she could touch the ground, I used the Blessing of Eloah and soared towards her swinging my arm but the Other Me pulled her legs in, throwing off my timing and avoided my strike.

She was as big as me but even with the Blessing of Eloah she was able to almost match my speed and she had a fighting style that I had not developed. My power was nothing if I could not hit her.

The Other Me swung her cloaked fist at me but I managed to dodge it and land a flying kick to her face. I grinned at the success, but the smile faded when I saw that she had been able to use her aura to cover her cheek where my foot had landed.

Using the Blessing of Eloah, I spun my body forward and brought my right foot down onto the Other Me's head and she was forced onto her knees.

My blows against her felt like they were against an actual person. She felt and seemed so alive, yet she spoke not one word to me as we fought.

She could manipulate her aura better than I could control my Faith and she had weakened my second blow too. I took a deep breath to calm myself and focused on my next attack.

I grabbed her by the shoulder of her dress and pulled her up and onto her feet. I intended to do this so I could get a better angle on her but before I could do anything the Other Me buried her fist in my gut as she rose.

The Blessing of Eloah weakened her attacks and although the attacks hurt, any damage they did was healed soon after.

It seemed a battle of attrition. I could continue to take her blows as they would be healed by the Blessing, but my Blessing would not last forever, and I still had to find Olympia and Hong Tao. The Other Me was fast, but I knew she had to be powered by something and if it was magic, it would not last forever either.

She punched me with her fist on the chin and I gasped as I bit my tongue and blood soaked my tongue before the Blessing of Eloah healed it.

She continued her barrage and swung her leg at me, and it landed in my stomach. Before she could pull her leg away, I grabbed it with my arms and then buried my right elbow into her leg while maintaining my grapple on her leg with my left arm.

As my elbow landed on her kneecap she let out a soundless cry of pain. I was glad she could feel pain. Using the Blessing of Eloah, I rose higher and lifted us into the air.

I flew towards the edge of the tower but before I could toss her off the side she grabbed onto the edge of the tower. I tugged on the Other Me's legs, urging my body to pull harder yet she remained in place.

The Other Me held on tight and I was unable to pull her away from the edge of the tower. She managed to remove her left foot, lifted it, and kicked me right in the nose.

There was a burst of white and black and then my sight flickered between the two. I lost my grip on the Other Me and when my vision returned, I saw that she had climbed up from the edge and was safely back on the tower floor.

As I touched my nose the Other Me used her aura to wrap me in it, pinning my arms to my sides. How could she Channel so proficiently?

I gasped as the Blessing of Eloah began healing my nose. It was broken and I could feel that both of my nostrils were blocked. There was a small *snap* as the power healed my nose, but it felt awkward on my face.

I had no time to focus on my nose as the Other Me pulled me in towards her. With my arms still restrained Other Me landed her fist into my right eye and I was momentarily blinded.

I groaned in pain, and I budged against the aura construct, pushing against it with all my might, and not even a second later it shattered, and the pieces of neon green light faded away before hitting the ground.

My eye went through a metamorphosis where one second it was swollen to the point that I could not see out of it and the next second the Blessing of Eloah took over and healed it and my vision was restored.

"Enough of this," I growled after blinking several times.

Melt I thought focusing on the Other Me, attempting to melt her as I had done the tower floors, but it seemed that the Blessing did not work on her.

"You are just a copy of me," I said as I soared towards her. "Anything you can do I can do better!"

The Other Me remained silent. Her eyes latched onto to me, and she raised her fists waiting for me to make my approach.

I focused on my sense of determination, and I brought forth my Faith. I lifted my hand and created an aura construct in the shape of a square as I had seen Savant do but instead using vertically to slice, I kept it horizontally and slammed it down onto the Other Me.

The Other Me was forced onto her stomach and narrowly avoided the aura construct. Even though I had missed her with the attack I smiled.

I had never created an aura construct although I had seen plenty of people do so since the destruction of Opulake. Now that I knew how I hoped my body and mind would remember when I lost the Blessing of Eloah.

It seemed most of the higher ranked Mystio could do it easily and even Odessa had made constructs in the Opulaki Church of Eloah against Samson during our fight for freedom.

I had managed to achieve it, but I felt it drain my magical reserves despite the Blessing of Eloah still cloaking me. I wonder if it required that much magic or if the Blessing was beginning to weaken.

Before the Other Me could stand I rose into the air and using my augmented strength I slammed my Faith covered foot into her head.

As my foot made contact her head burst like a melon expelling silver gunk and her form melted into a dirty brown sludge on the tower floor.

I bent over onto my knees and tried to catch my breath. I inhaled through my nose and sighed deeply.

I thought about my friend Odessa once more and smiled. I could have given her a fair fight now with the Blessing of Eloah. I wanted her to see me shine and I hoped I would be able to use the Blessing more in the future.

It was common belief that those who received the Blessing of Eloah only received it once but that was not always the case with prophets.

Arugula Balthazar, the Third Prophet of Eloah, had been known to use the Blessing of Eloah whenever she wished, often using it to complete menial tasks.

There was also Langston Bao, the Nineteenth Prophet of Eloah, who could only use the Blessing on the sixth day of the week, but he could use the Blessing of Eloah every week if he pleased. It was for that reason that Friday was when he did his patrols, missions, and sermons.

There had been prophets who had never been seen yielding the Blessing such as Allegra Gene and even though she was a good prophet some did not recognize her authority because of it.

I shuddered at the thought of Isla Fabiola who had only wielded the Blessing of Eloah as a child and had never demonstrated it again in her life.

If the Return was soon then Eloah would need me as his prophet. Surely, he would continue to allow me to conduct his power in the future.

I was grateful for the power, but my thoughts turned to Estella. I wished that she could have seen me shine too. If Eloah had intervened before now, she could. Why had he waited so long?

If only Eloah had given his Blessing to any of the other Opulakis. They could have used this power to defeat Samson. They were all Children of his and good people.

Why me? I wondered. Estella had done the same trainings I had. Tripa Fons knew every hymn and scripture of Eloah. Yet he had let the both of them die and had given his Blessing to me.

I could not see his Vision.

His plan did not make sense. If he had given his Blessing to an Opulaki when we had rebelled against Lord Laurens or even when the First Constellation had attacked then he would not need me now as his tool of vengeance.

There would have been no need for vengeance and my friends and family would still be alive and all the more grateful for his interference.

I sighed although there was no one there to hear me. It was not my place to question Eloah. I knew his Vision was from a perspective I could not see from.

I glanced at the pyramid once more and after another sigh I floated over to it and landed in front of it. I saw a perforation and saw that the capstone opened.

I flipped the tip of the pyramid open and saw a small circular basin with a hole in the middle of it. I did not know how I knew the *imperi* was in it, but I did.

I glanced at the sink contraption. At a closer inspection I saw a small prick. I touched my finger on it and blood burst from my skin and lazily dripped down the sink and into the hole.

Suddenly there was a loud vibration and a moment later the tower of magic was no longer underground and instead we were not in a booming jungle.

Arabella and the Tower of Magic

After the overwhelming quiet that claimed the city of Jormondor the jungle roared with the loudness of a thousand person festival.

I rushed to the edge of the tower and saw a verdant world of plant life below us. It was filled to the brim with life. I had never seen a jungle, but it was amazing.

The darkness of the cavern had been replaced with the light of Astria. Zaniah had not yet risen but even Astria alone was enough to irritate my eyes after they had been in the darkness for so long.

Relief for my eyes came quickly as a giant stick bug emerged in front of me and blocked out Astria's light, leaving me in its shadow.

I had never seen one so large. It was larger than I. It was larger even than Eloah and was taller than the tower of magic itself.

Its skin was a glossy teal and it had big maroon wings. The wings were etched with veins that were dark shades of red. Although the wings were large, they seemed too small to actually lift the giant stick bug into the air to fly.

Its eyes looked at me and it let out a scream that drilled into my head and I was forced to cover my eyes to reduce its blare.

I yelled and flew towards the pyramid and tried to figure out how to activate it. I knew there was a correlation between it and my appearance here in the jungle, but I was not sure exactly what had triggered it.

I quickly grew frustrated. I glanced up at the giant insect. Its long antennae twitched as if it were agitated, and its mouth was surrounded by pincers that were the size of a grown man.

With a grunt I plunged my hand into the pyramid and pried the top off. I took the basin and threw it onto the tower floor.

The pyramid was no longer pristine and instead looked decrepit with jagged pieces of metal protruding in several directions.

Sitting on its side in the pyramid was a band of the black metal enclosed around a ring of a white gem that glowed with a purple sheen.

At its sight I knew that it was a true *imperi* not a false one or an illusion like before. It appeared even different from the one Hua had shown that was black, yet many colors.

I bit my bottom lip in anticipation and reached for the *imperi* but just before my fingers could touch it an arrow shot towards me.

I managed to dodge the attack and looked up to see Hong Tao holding a bow with a notched arrow. Olympia leaned against a nearby battlement with a sly smile on her face.

They were not concerned with the giant insect that was lumbering towards us with their eyes on me and the *imperi.*

I *was* quite worried about the bug. I had never seen any creature so large, yet I could not afford to look behind me. All I could do was watch its shadow move and grow larger as it approached us.

I kept my eyes on the First Constellation bandits as they took a step towards me, and Olympia's smile was so wide it made me sick.

"Thank you for your assistance," she said showing off her bright white teeth. "What did I say, Hong Tao? Hook, line, sinker." Hong Tao nodded his head although he did not smile as she did.

"Hook, line, and sinker," he repeated.

Chapter THIRTEEN

hong tao

Despite the danger the two leaders of the First Constellation posed and the giant insect behind me I could not help but laugh.

"I have been chasing after you two, worried you would do something disastrous, but you have been waiting for me this whole time?" I said.

"We had not been able to open the pyramid and expected that the Mystio would be able to do so. I had not expected you would be the one to assist us. I did not see you use these powers against Samson. How did you become so much stronger in a matter of days? It seems both you *and* Odessa are special," Olympia said with a smile.

It was astonishing that they had manipulated me so easily. They had not been able to retrieve the *imperi* themselves, so they had brought us here to have us do it for them.

Their scheme had worked so far but I had no further plans to do as they expected, and Olympia's nonchalance irritated me.

She spoke about us as if we were game pieces. What did she know of my friend Odessa? It was I who had shared the empathy link with her. I had experienced her memories and lived through them as if I was Odessa herself.

"You have no right to speak about Odessa," I said. "You know nothing about her."

"I know more about her than you," Olympia said with a wide smile, but I was tired of the sound of her voice.

Using the Blessing of Eloah, I quickly picked up the *imperi* and slipped it on my finger. Hong Tao fired three more arrows and I managed to deflect two and then catch the third with my right hand before throwing it on the tower floor.

The *imperi* tightened around my finger, and I saw that though my ring finger was almost completely restored though I felt no different. With a groan I realized I did not know how to use the magical item.

I just wanted us to return to the city of Jormondor. I did not know if I could focus on both bandits and the stick bug behind me at once.

I lifted the bowl and quickly pricked my finger once more. I focused on the thought of returning to Jormondor.

The tower vibrated in response and after I blinked I saw that we had returned to the glow lit cavern once more. Jormondor sat below us, and I was glad we had left the green stick bug behind in the jungle.

"How did you do that?" Olympia asked. "Blood magic?"

The golden glow of the tower began to return to its original black tone resonating from the pyramid that had held the *imperi* and flowing downwards. It was the opposite effect to when the gold had first coated the tower.

"The two of you can not defeat me," I said. "I have the Blessing of Eloah and you will not be able to match me. I am his prophet and his vengeance against you," I said. "I have the *imperi* and will use it to destroy the both of you."

"Where is Eloah's so called vengeance?" Olympia said with a sneer. "Let's see it!"

I soared through the air towards the two of them. Hong Tao fired three arrows at me quickly. Two of them pierced me, one in my right shoulder and the other in my right thigh but the third I avoided by lowering my head and ducking it.

I groaned in pain as the arrows punctured my skin. In the moment my head was lowered to avoid the final arrow I felt pain as Hong Tao extended his arm out, gripped the arrow, and pulled it out of my thigh.

I cried out as the arrowhead emerged, leaving a puncture wound in my leg. The Blessing of Eloah began healing the wound, but it was slower than it had been before.

I was wondering if it was beginning to fade. I had done amazing magical feats and I did not look forward to losing the power. I needed to end this fight quickly just in case. There was no time to soak in my vengeance and triumph as I had fantasized.

Hong Tao pulled his arm back quickly and stabbed towards me with the arrow tight in his hand, but I crossed my arms into an X and manifested my Faith. The arrowhead bounced off of my neon green Faith and the wooden shaft shattered.

Maintaining my concentration, I sent my Faith onto my arm and swung my forearm at Hong Tao, but he caught my blow with his forearm.

We pushed against each other, and I flew backward several feet while Hong Tao was only knocked back a single step.

I levitated forward and swung at him with my fist flying upward, but Hong Tao ducked low and avoided my hand. I threw my other hand downwards, but Hong Tao leaned backward, and I missed again.

He twisted his body and swung his right fist towards me, but I caught it with my Faith cloaked forearm. I saw surprise in his eyes for a moment before his face returned to his expressionless default.

Despite this Hong Tao pulled harshly at my arm and it swung down and open against my will. With his right hand he punched his fist into my chest directly above my heart and I felt it flutter.

I felt the force of it and even with the Blessing of Eloah cloaking me it hurt. If not for the Blessing the blow may have killed me; I could not let him hit me like that anymore.

I coughed and touched the arrow in my shoulder. I didn't want to risk not having my hands available to counter or attack. I also didn't want to experience the pain of Hong Tao yanking it out so I quickly broke the wood near my skin but left the arrowhead in until I could carefully remove it.

I leaned forward and aimed my fist towards Hong Tao's gut, but he was ready and caught me by the wrist and when I reached to remove his hand, he gripped my other wrist too.

With his hands gripping both of my wrists tightly he pulled me out of the air and towards the ground and then kneed me deeply in the gut.

I yelped in pain and attempted to fly away, but Hong Tao pulled me forward and spun me around in a circle once and released my left hand.

The maneuver left me off balance. Hong Tao kicked at my left leg, sending my knee forward and I began to fall but I was able to levitate before my knee hit the ground.

While I focused on coming up with a counterattack Hong Tao buried his left foot in my gut. As I groaned in pain he pushed me away, pulled his bow from his back, and fired an arrow at me.

I lifted my arm and swiped my hand through the air and sent the arrow clattering onto the floor with a wave of wind.

I attempted to focus on Hong Tao, but he was gone. My eyes searched for him, but I only saw Olympia leaning against the wall.

She lifted her hand and waved, and I scowled at her. The expression felt awkward on my face. Olympia smiled in response and then with an expression of mock surprise she pointed behind me.

I turned just in time to catch Hong Tao in a spell. I exuded a burst of frost that coated my body and clothing white, and a cloud of icy mist burst from me.

The burst of magic coated Hong Tao and froze him in place. It was only for a second, but it was enough for me to dodge his lunge.

Melt I thought and pointed at the tower floor just below Hong Tao's feet. The tower floor obeyed my command and melted revealing the floor below us.

Hong Tao somehow managed to jump backward to avoid falling in, but I was buffeted by a burst of hot air coming from below.

I was blinded for a moment and in that second, I felt Hong Tao slip the *imperi* off of my finger. I attempted to close my hand to stop him, but it was difficult and after a momentary struggle Hong Tao was successful.

"Olympia," Hong Tao said, and he threw the *imperi* toward her and she snatched it out of the air and smiled at it.

"No!" I cried.

I heard a cry from below me and I saw Savant, Micah, Hua, and the twins on the floor underneath us. They were combatting a large lizard that exhaled hot air from its mouth at them that left burn marks on the tower floor.

Nearby were the corpses of two other lizards. The one they faced looked like it was the last one, but the others looked exhausted.

Even Lancer Savant Solace slouched slightly as the lizard creature made its approach toward them. I looked up for Hong Tao and Olympia, but they had vanished.

"No!" I shouted and rose into the air looking for any sign of the First Constellation leaders but there were no clues as to where they had gone.

I had only looked away for a moment yet that was enough for them to silently escape. How could they vanish so quickly? I couldn't let them get away. Eloah had chosen me alone for this task. There was no one else. I was the last Daughter of Opulake.

I flew back down to the hole that revealed the floor before me. The Mystio and the others appeared to be on their last leg against the lizard. Frey lay limply on the tower floor with Micah leaning over him and I could see Freya yelling something at her brother.

"I have to help them," I said softly, but before I could descend, I heard Eloah's voice in my head as if it was Odessa through our empathy link.

"No, leave them!" Eloah said. **"They are no children of mine. You were chosen for vengeance! Pursue the First Constellation! Kill them!"**

I looked around once more and realized the First Constellation would be attempting to escape and the only way to do that was with the submarine we had arrived in.

With my new speed and strength, I should have been able to catch up to them and stop them before they reached the submarine.

I heard Hua cry out and looked over just in time to see her get blasted with a burst of stifling air from the lizard's maw.

"I have to help them," I said once more and began to descend through the air towards the party.

"Arabella, if you continue you will lose my Blessing and you may never be able to be a conduit for it again," Eloah said. **"As my next Prophet your job is to protect my children and these friends of yours do not worship me. The Mystio can not be trusted to deal justice, they have already failed thrice."**

I heard his words, but I ignored them.

Could I do that? Ignore who I had spent my whole life worshipping?

Would I still be his Prophet?

Would I lose the Blessing?

Could Arabella of Opulake even help the Mystio and the others without the Blessing of Eloah?

I soared downwards toward the giant lizard as it rounded on Savant. Even though I approached the lizard from behind it spotted me somehow and swung its tail towards me.

Arabella and the Tower of Magic

I caught the lizard's rough tail with one hand but the moment my hand made contact; I could feel the Blessing of Eloah fading quickly.

I gripped the snake's tail and with a deep breath I lifted the lizard into the air and careful not to hurt anyone I slammed the lizard onto the tower floor.

The lizard howled as his head banged onto the hard ground and its spine arced in pain letting me know it was still alive.

It pulled against my grip, but I held on tight. There was a wet snapping sound, and I was left holding the wriggling tail of the lizard.

The lizard had detached its tail and I watched as the stub where its tail had been began to regenerate. The lizard spun quickly and then jumped towards me.

As it flew through the air it opened its mouth wide open and its breath began to burn me. The temperature skyrocketed making it hard to focus.

I groaned in pain and fell to my knees. My skin began to bubble. I felt blisters rise up and subsequently burst and the lizard aimed its jaw towards my head, ready to snap me up.

Suddenly the heat abated and there was an explosion of blood and bordeaux magic. I saw now that the lizard's head had been pierced by an aura arrow fired by Savant who held a bow made of pure magic.

It must have taken some skill for him to land the shot while he was wounded and while the lizard had been in motion.

I preferred bows to swords or daggers. They had range and could be safely used from a distance. We had not had much time with weapons growing up but the few times I had used a bow my arms had been too weak to effectively manage the bow.

The lizard's body fell onto the tower floor with a wet *smack*. I watched it in amazement because although the lizard was no doubt dead, its tail continued to regrow itself slowly for several seconds before its progress was halted leaving the tail only partially regenerated.

"Arabella," Micah said in greeting, and I turned away from the lizard to face them.

They knelt over Frey and Hua who were both burned to where their skin was tinged red and the flesh beneath the surface of their skin could be seen in several blotches across their bodies.

I felt nowhere near as strong as I had been, but I still possessed vestiges of the Blessing of Eloah. My own skin was beginning to heal via the Blessing, and I could feel cool relief setting in.

I flew towards Micah only a few inches before my power of flight faded and my bare feet landed in a puddle of hot lizard blood.

It seemed the clothing had been part of the Blessing also. I was left without the brown sandals and in the green dress I had been in before. I was glad to see that the tears were gone and I was glad to not be covered in filth anymore.

I ran over to Micah's side and knelt over Frey and Hua. Freya had her arms on Frey's chest, and she sobbed quietly. As I got closer, I saw that his chest no longer rose from breath.

Hua looked as if she was burned worse, but I could see she was breathing still so she at least was still alive.

I could feel the rest of the Blessing of Eloah's power fading quickly and knew I could hesitate no longer.

"Bring them closer," I instructed and with Micah and Freya's help Hua and Freya were laid side by side and I knelt in between the two.

I could not help but feel guilty. Yes, Hua had left me after the hell hound attack but it was not the Elohan way to get even. We were taught to always move with compassion.

If I had not left the others behind they would not be injured now and the First Constellation would still have been waiting on us. We could have fought them together.

With a sigh I placed one of my hands on each of their shoulders and thought *heal*. I felt the spell draining me as the magic entered their bodies. It was not painful but felt uncomfortable.

It was wonderous to watch the Blessing at work. It spread faster than normal magical healing and in only a second or two Hua and Frey's bodies were restored to their best condition.

Hua's eyes moved under her eyelids, but she remained unconscious. Frey on the other hand still did not draw breath despite his body's restoration.

With Hua healed I placed both of my hands on Frey; one on his shoulder and one on his chest.

Heal! I commanded.

I felt the rest of Eloah's Blessing leave me and the black glyphs that coated my skin faded. The Blessing was gone, and I felt like Arabella of Opulake once more yet still Frey did not move.

"Do not give up, Frey Lunaredi," I said.

The Blessing of Eloah had faded yet I still had my Faith. I had met Eloah, he was real, he had chosen me as his next Prophet. I focused on my belief and my neon green Faith appeared.

I pressed firmly on Frey once more and with a healing intent I focused on healing Frey's body, but it seemed all injuries on his body had already been repaired. Healing any further would not help him and would be a waste of Faith.

I lifted my hands and shook my head at Freya who had been watching me intently.

Her sobs returned but this time they were not quiet, she let her pain out in loud whimpers as she laid her head on her brother's chest.

Micah placed their hand on my shoulder and squeezed it slightly.

"You did all you could," they said.

"If I had not left—" I started but Savant interrupted me.

"We can not focus on what ifs and maybes," he said. His uniform had several cuts in it revealing his skin and undergarments and his Mystio chest piece had a large scorch mark on the middle that had burned several letters of "Mystio" off.

I closed my eyes and exhaled deeply. This was my fault. I had let my emotions get the best of me and now Frey had died.

Eloah, please give me the power to heal Frey Lunaredi I prayed. *I promise I will make sure the Elohans of Opulake are avenged. Samson, Hong Tao, Olympia, and Jesuit, they will all face your justice.*

Eloah did not reply, he had never done so before today but I gasped as I saw my normal neon green Faith flicker and transition to a golden yellow aura that exuded warmth and gave off a scent of vanilla.

I touched Frey's chest just above his heart and the instant my fingers touched his shirt his eyes burst open. His blue eyes glowed neon green like mine had been, but it lasted only a second before returning to their normal pale blue shade.

My aura faded quickly and although I held my hand up and tried to manifest it once more to see if it was still golden, it refused to return.

I saw now that only one of my fingers had been restored. My ring finger was back to normal but there was a small nub where my pinky should have been.

My thoughts were interrupted as I heard Eloah's voice in my mind once more.

I have granted your request. Do not fail me, Prophet. My vengeance is death.

Chapter FOURTEEN

imperi

I did not feel tired but with the Blessing of Eloah gone I felt diminished, like I was only a part of who I should have been.

Once it was clear the others were in no danger I stood up and looked towards the next floor. It would no doubt be faster to go up to escape the tower instead of descending back the way from which we had come.

"We need to go," I said to Savant. "They have the *imperi* and I believe they mean to return to the submarine."

"I feared as much when I saw the gold on the walls and floors return to black," Savant said.

I quickly gave the Mystio and the others a quick summary of the events that had transpired since I had left them behind. I saw their expressions as I spoke, and they ranged from worry to amazement to regret but at no point while I spoke did I see anger.

Savant glanced at Frey who was studying Hua who still lay unconscious on the tower floor. Freya was close behind Frey watching him. Freya was speechless at her brother's revival and her eyes wandered across his body looking for any signs of injury but there were none.

Micah looked at me with a question on their face, but they did not ask it. I wondered what the question was, and it gnawed at me.

I did not know why I cared so much about what they thought of me, but I wanted to seem like a kind and holy person; more than seem like it I wanted to *be* a kind and holy person. I had no doubt made myself seem like less of a woman when I had left them behind.

"We aren't fit for a pursuit mission," Savant said finally. "We must make sure these civilians are cared for. We will return to Opulake to transport the remaining bandits to Fort Mudo. We will have to plan a retrieval mission for the *imperi*."

"No!" Both Micah and I said at the same time. "What about Samson and the *imperi?*" I asked.

"From what you told me, the distance between us and them will be too far for us to hope to catch up with them. We must figure out a way to escape here on our own."

"Can you not create a bridge of magic from the tower to where we entered the city?" I asked. "That would save us so much time."

"I alone could not. The distance is too far, and the duration would be too long to maintain while we crossed. Even though I believe between the three of us we could Channel far enough to conjure the aura bridge construct you envision, the effort to maintain it while we crossed would cost us much magic and we will struggle even more with our foes. They are well rested, and we are well worn," Savant answered.

"I will not retreat, is that what you think of me?" Hua said. Her voice startled me. Her brown eyes looked up from her position on the tower floor.

She still lay on her back, but after she spoke, she slowly leaned forward and stood. Her body was free of injuries she looked deep into my eyes.

Without rising she said, "Thank you for your assistance. I am in your debt. Together, we can defeat my father, can I lend you my strength?"

"You are welcome," I said with a nod, and Hua rose until she was standing upright once more.

"I am sorry for leaving you behind also," I said. I looked her back into the eyes so she knew I meant it but she only laughed.

"Let's just call it even, why don't we?" Hua said and I nodded.

I looked from Hua to Savant and could see he was thinking. His eyes studied each of us and finally his eyes landed on Micah.

"And you're in agreeance, Micah?" Savant asked.

Micah nodded.

"I am, Lancer Solace," Micah said, using Savant's formal title and last name as they normally did.

"Okay," Savant relented. "*Ase Vertan.*"

"*Ase Vertan,*" Micah and I said.

Savant raised both of his palms and a bordeaux colored disk appeared beneath the six of us.

"Get closer," Micah said and as we did so Savant Channeled his aura to decrease in size and allow him to use less energy.

Savant raised his hands and the platform he had constructed rose into the air as we made our way to the hole above us that I had dissolved with the Blessing of Eloah.

Savant slowed his approach and Micah climbed through the hole. They then extended an arm down to us. Freya glanced at Frey as if to make sure he would not vanish and then gripped Micah's hand and they pulled her through first.

Freya rotated and together she and Micah helped Frey up. Hua took a step up next but hesitated and then looked at me.

"You should go first Arabella, don't you think?" she said gesturing towards the twins and Micah.

"No, go ahead. I am the heaviest, I should go last," I said.

Hua hesitated for a second, then she turned away, gripped the hands of Micah and Freya, and was pulled up and through the hole.

I glanced back at Savant, but he gestured for me to go forward with his head.

"Go ahead," he said. "It will be easier to maintain this from down here."

I nodded and looked upwards towards the rest.

"Are you ready? You all may need to help lift me," I said as my face blushed in embarrassment.

"Not at all," Micah said with a smile, the first smile they had given me since I had come back, and I felt my cheeks burning.

"I can lift you all by myself," Micah said and without using their aura they gripped my good hand and pulled me up through the hole without any help.

I felt my heart racing and I looked at Micah, but they were looking down at Savant. Savant raised the platform and standing completely straight he rose through the hole in the floor and stepped lightly onto the tower floor.

I glanced at the destroyed pyramid that had contained the *imperi*. They would not have the *imperi* now if I had not retrieved it for them. If they got away with it and people were hurt by it, it would be my fault.

"Aura bridge next, let's move, people," Savant shouted, and we all ran to the edge of the tower.

"Let me do this," Micah said.

Micah began to speak once more in that foreign dialect, and I watched as their golden brown eyes began to glow white once more.

They levitated and pointed their hands at the edge of the tower. From the tower's edge, the ice began to form, and it shot downwards towards the edge of the dwarven city.

It looked like a slide that would have been seen in Opulake during the Opulaki Moon Festival except it had no cart nor safety rails to keep us from plummeting to the ground. It was also much larger and longer.

Once the bridge was completed Micah gasped as they fell straight onto their knees. I rushed towards them, but they coughed and told us to go forward with their hand.

"Reverse lead, I'll go first, Micah you take the rear," Savant said.

Without a further word Savant rushed forward and jumped onto the ice bridge with no fear. What was left of his cape billowed open as he surfed down the bridge and towards the tunnel that led to the submarine.

"Woah," Freya gasped. "He sure knows how to pose."

She glanced at Frey to make sure he was alright and then climbed onto the ice bridge. Instead of surfing it like Savant had, Freya sat and pushed her body forward with her arms and slid after Savant with a sound of cheer.

Frey was assisted by Hua and because he looked so frightened, she climbed up behind him and wrapped her arms around him.

She molded his body into a kneeling position and then knelt behind him. It was interesting to see considering their size difference and together they descended after Savant and Freya leaving only Micah and I left on the tower of magic.

I glanced at Micah with concern. They were still on their knees and their breathing was slower and deeper than usual. They saw me watching and they gave me a strained smile.

"Go ahead, Arabella," they said. "I will be right behind you."

I nodded my head and climbed onto the ice bridge. The ice was colder than expected and my bare feet burned from the touch of it.

Here," Micah said, and they tore the bottom of their shirt and then ripped it into two pieces. They stood slowly and made their way to where I stood.

"Here," they said, and I raised my right foot, and they wrapped it in the cloth from their shirt and then repeated the process with my left.

The cloth did not fully numb the cold, but it helped immensely. I smiled at Micah, and they smiled back.

"Thank you," I said, and Micah simply nodded in answer.

I turned towards the ice bridge and shivered against my will. It was a steady descent, and I could see the others in the distance waving to me to come towards them.

I pulled my body onto the ice bridge and was buffeted by the wind as gravity pulled me forward and down. My hair was flung behind me and the skin on my face felt stretched by the force of the descent.

The bridge curved slightly and if I had not leaned my body the opposite way to compensate I would have been flung off and become a human pancake.

I continued to build up speed as I approached the end of the ice bridge, and I had no idea how I would stop. I flew towards the twins, Savant, and Hua and yelled, "I don't know how to stop!"

As I approached them Savant Channeled his aura into something that resembled a large cushion and despite my expectations of the aura construct being hard and solid, it was soft and slowed me down and caught me.

"You must be very skilled to change the form of your aura," I said to Savant.

"I have had a long time to practice," he replied, his eyes trained on Micah as they approached.

Micah let their speed take them and trusted Savant to slow them. Savant did not fail them and as Micah reached the end of the ice bridge Savant caught them with his aura as he had caught me.

"Do you just leave this here?" I asked Micah referring to the ice slide and they shrugged.

"It would be even more work to break it down," Micah replied.

I glanced at the ice bridge once more. The city of Jormondor was a prettier view when it did not contain the First Constellation. I had never seen such an impressive city and it was possible I never would again.

My thoughts shifted to Lady Gorin. I hoped she would not be lonely in the ghost city. I knew what being the last of home felt like but I could not imagine spending the rest of my life in the ruins of Opulake.

"Okay let's go," Savant said and together we turned away from the fallen city of Jormondor.

The trek through the tunnel upwards and back towards the submarine seemed to take less time than it had taken to get to Jormondor.

I knew our chances of catching the bandits before they departed were low, yet I took deep breaths and focused on running as fast as I could.

Despite this, Frey and I trailed the others. I was surprised he had the same pace as me since he was the tallest out of all of us and his long legs should have made running an easy task. Perhaps it was his recent encounter with death; I was sure death took its toll on a person.

"Jump!" I heard Savant yell from in front of me and in the dim light I saw the body of Lady Gorin's metal dog, Canus.

Its eyes were no longer lit, and it looked as if it had been torn in two at its jaw leaving several cords of some type of sparking metal exposed.

Had Lady Gorin decided to help? Had my words swayed her?

"Up ahead!" Savant yelled and I steeled myself.

The closer we got the brighter it got, and I could feel the temperature rising also. Sweat began to form on my forehead and soon my dress was drenched.

I saw something large looming ahead of us and I thought of the giant stick bug I had seen but the creature in front of me was large but much smaller than the stick bug.

As we came to the clearing we had arrived at I saw with surprise that the submarine remained but there was an even bigger surprise awaiting us.

I saw Hong Tao, Olympia, and Samson fighting against Lady Gorin alone. Her hands streaked through the sky and above her made of pure fire was a winged creature that exuded heat and dripped liquid flames.

Micah appeared at my side, and they reassuringly gripped my shoulder.

"What is that?" I asked.

Micah was silent for a moment before they spoke and when they did their voice cracked.

"It's a dragon."

Chapter FIFTEEN

odessa

I had heard tales of dragons.

They were large lizards with wings and the ability to cough fire from their mouths. Their claws were sharp as daggers and there skin as hard as stone. They could fly and it took over a hundred fighters to defeat just one, if they could reach the creature at all.

I had also heard that the last dragon had been killed by dwarves during the war between humans and dwarves. I could not believe there was one here with us in the dwarven city.

Why would that be if the dwarves were the ones who had killed the last one?

But the dragon above us did not blow fire, it *was* fire. It illuminated the cavern as if Astria and Zaniah themselves were below ground with us cloaking us in a crimson glow.

The dragon appeared to be the result of some sort of fire magic and was being completely controlled by Lady Gorin.

When her hands and fingers twitched the dragon responded as if Lady Gorin was some magnificent puppet master.

"Lady Gorin!" I called and she looked at me and smiled.

"Arabella of Opulake," she called. "Join me in my final battle and we shall smite these desperados together. Criminals such as these do not deserve the inheritance of my kin."

It seemed the dwarven woman had completely changed her mind from when I had last seen her. I had thought she would be upset about the death of her metal dog but if she was, she did not show it. I wondered if she had come because of duty or because of my words.

As the Prophet of Eloah, I would soon have to address the entirety of Eloah's Children and I wanted to know if I had a persuasive voice. I would save the thought for another time.

Hong Tao dodged a particularly large glob of liquid fire that dripped from the dragon's belly. He furrowed his brow and I saw his face was beaded with sweat.

The glob of fire that he had dodged splashed onto the ground and steamed behind him near his bow. I saw his bow broken and smoking, and he was left with nothing to fight with but his hands.

Olympia's clothes were scorched black in several places as if she had not been as adept as Hong Tao in dodging the fire.

I allowed myself a small smile and was glad to see that the smile she loved to wear was gone and there was a nasty looking bite mark on her arm.

Good one, Canus I thought.

Samson for his part was inching away slowly towards the submarine. He moved as if he was not over six feet tall and was hoping no one would notice him retreating.

I locked eyes with him, and he scowled at me but made no attempt to approach me. There was no way I would let him get away.

"Micah and Arabella, you handle Samson," Savant called. "Frey and Freya please do your best to stall or detain Olympia. "Hua, you're with me. We will assist Lady Gorin with Hong Tao."

I was glad he had assigned me to fight Samson. Olympia or Hong Tao may have had the *imperi* but what

I owed Samson was personal. They were all on my list, but I wanted to prove I had grown stronger by beating Samson.

"Heard," Micah said and then looked at me.

I had also wanted to take down Hong Tao. He had bested me in the tower of magic. I owed him a rematch but without the Blessing of Eloah I doubted I would have been able to do much against him but get in the way of Savant and the others.

Still, it was Lady Gorin who had created the dragon and she would have Lancer Savant Solace to help them along with Hua, Hong Tao's own daughter.

If anyone knew his weakness it would be her. They made a good team and I doubted they would need me, but I was left unsatisfied and a little hurt.

I would have even settled for a bout with Olympia. She had manipulated me. She spoke much but I had yet to see her really fight.

Perhaps she was more a woman of intellect than fist. After all, it had been her plan to use me as a tool to unlock the *imperi* for her and Hong Tao.

I needed to know why she was interested in my friend Odessa. She had asked me about her on the submarine and then let me go, but that act was probably all according to plan for her.

Why? She was a puppet master of a different sort and I struggled to see where her strings went. Her plan, whatever it was, seemed to involve Odessa too.

"Let's go, Arabella," Micah said, breaking my train of thought. I nodded my head, dismissing any thoughts that would not help me beat Samson.

The dragon cut low through the air towards Samson, and he was forced to drop onto his stomach to avoid the flames, yet his loincloth still burst into flames. He yelped in pain and he jumped into the water to quell the fire.

As we neared where he had dived, I saw Samson had begun to swim towards the submarine. Micah stood at the water's edge, thrust his hand forward, and wrapped an aura construct around Samson's body.

Micah lifted Samson's body and with a small grunt he threw him onto the cavern floor away from the water and the submarine.

Samson sputtered for a moment and then quickly rose to his feet. Looking at him now it was hard to imagine that he was the one who had destroyed my home.

The Bane of Opulake appeared pathetic. He stood up tall, yet he looked small. This could not have been the man that had killed Tripa Fons and Estella. It could not have been the cruel man who had sneered and bragged about how my mentor had died.

Tripa Fons and Estella had carried themselves with pride and had been faithful Children of Eloah; yet Eloah had not intervened to save them. He had directed me to be his vessel for vengeance.

I had seen Micah defeat Samson once before. I had beaten him before with Odessa's help. I needed to do this myself if I wanted to be the next Prophet of Eloah. I needed to be stronger than I had been.

"I have got this," I told Micah. "Go help Savant and the others."

I did not take my eyes off of Samson, but I could hear the doubt in Micah's voice when they asked, "Are you sure, Arabella?"

Still not looking back I said, "*Ase Vertan.*"

"I believe in you," they said. "*Ase Vertan,*" Micah replied, and I heard their footsteps depart.

Samson sneered at me. As Micah left, he seemed to grow more confident. He even felt comfortable enough to talk trash again. I would use his comfort to my advantage.

"This won't go like the arena. I will kill you and then that other brat and her sister are next," he spat at me as he cracked his fingers.

I did not reply. I knew he only meant to upset me and lower my guard. I had fallen for it before. I wish he would get some new tricks.

I took a deep breath and blinked. I attempted to call forth the Blessing of Eloah but did not feel the immense power that I had felt before.

I did not expect it to be mastered so easily so I was not surprised. I focused on my faith in Eloah and my Faith appeared around my body, but it was quite different than it had been before.

Gone was the neon green light I had been blessed with my whole life. It was replaced by the golden glow I had seen when I had revived Frey. Perhaps Eloah's power still lingered.

I took a deep breath and the golden aura expanded and shimmered around me. I could hear the others fighting around me. They would not fail, and neither would I.

"I am the Vengeance of Eloah," I said looking Samson in the eyes and gesturing for him to come forward.

Samson roared and rushed towards me. He was as fast as I remembered. It had caught me off guard in Opulake, but this was not Opulake.

If Odessa were there, she would have started by tossing sand in her adversary's face to throw them off guard, but I figured Samson would expect it and the ground was too hard and non-granular to do that attack efficiently.

I would beat him just as my friend Odessa had. *I would be the hurricane and I would blow down Samson with my Faith and avenge those he had slaughtered.*

Instead of grabbing sand as Odessa had done in the Opulaki Church of Eloah, I used my Faith to dig into the cavern and gripped large chunks of the ground.

Samson did not slow at my use of magic but I was ready for his head on approach. He would not catch me off guard again.

As Samson neared I managed to pull two large rocks out of the ground with my Faith and I propelled them towards Samson. One rock was caught by Samson with his large hands and thrown onto the ground but the other slammed into Samson's head and burst into a cloud of dust and smaller stones, yet he continued coming towards me.

He got into arm range and brought his fist down towards my chest, but I cloaked my arms and caught Samson's arms just under his wrists.

I jumped off the ground to lift his arms and the maneuver seemed to take Samson by surprise. He lost his balance and stumbled backwards. I rushed forward and with my arms still cloaked I punched him in the stomach.

"That was for Tripa Fons," I said.

He let out a satisfying groan of pain but as he doubled over from the pain, he gripped me at the waist with his hands and lifted.

"Woah!" I yelled as I was pulled off of the ground and lost my sense of gravity as Samson lifted me up and threw me through the air behind him.

It was different from the Blessing of Eloah and although I was only in the air for a few seconds before I hit the ground with an almighty crash. I bit my tongue again but harder this time and tasted blood immediately.

I no longer had the Blessing of Eloah to heal myself so I couldn't allow myself to get more injuries in this fight. It was possible that I would have to face Hong Tao and Olympia next.

My shoulder felt bruised, but I could hear Samson's large feet slamming against the ground as he worked to close the distance between us, so I ignored the pain and quickly climbed onto my feet.

As I stood, my eyes searched for the bandit and found him only inches away and he slammed his fist into my chest.

I groaned in pain and coughed. My hands instinctively reached to touch the injured area and while I did that Samson buried both of his fists into my gut one after another causing me to stumble back in an attempt to put distance between us, but Samson did not let me retreat.

He aimed a fist towards my face, but I managed to trip backwards and avoid the blow but in doing so I fell backwards onto my butt.

He was moving too quickly for me to counter or conjure my Faith. I tried to control my breathing, but dodging was taking too much of my focus.

Samson lifted his large foot and attempted to stomp me, but I quickly spread my legs and his foot landed in between them.

He looked at me, his face a mask of surprise. It seemed he still was underestimating me.

I took a deep breath, cloaked my hand, and slammed it into his leg. Samson howled and I jumped to my feet while he was distracted.

"That was for Eufaula O'Connor," I said.

I wrapped my arms around Samson's torso and threw myself against him, hoping to push him onto the ground with me on top of him, but he was too strong.

He managed to stay upright and began to slam his fists into my back. The blows were numbed by my Faith initially, but it was not long before the aura construct began to crack.

I did not have energy to spare to reinforce it, so I was forced to release my grip on him but not before he slammed his fists into my back once more. The aura construct shattered, and I was forced to the ground.

My back ached and I rolled away quickly before he could stomp me and raised myself onto my feet. Using my Faith had drained me, and I was trying to catch my breath when Samson slammed his fist into my stomach.

I crashed onto my back and Samson slammed his foot onto my left hand. I heard one of my fingers crack and I screamed in agony as Samson smiled down at me.

I looked for Micah in the distance, but my eyes could not find them. I saw that the dragon of fire was gone but I saw nothing more.

I climbed onto my knees just as Samson slammed his foot into my shoulder, and I was plunged into the water and the ocean's icy embrace snatched me and pulled me under.

The light faded and I was left in darkness.

PART TWO

Pershing Aiguo "Micah" Zhang

Chapter SIXTEEN

micah

Arabella was gone.

I had seen her fall into the water, and she had not yet emerged. I shifted my stance to go help her but thought better of it.

We had been bending the rules this whole mission and my number one priority was Hong Tao. As a Mystio I had to focus on the kingdom first.

I had agreed thinking she would use the Elohan Faith Magic she had used before but it had not appeared to manifest.

I worried about her chances of success while she faced Samson alone, but it was out of my hands now. I had faith that she would do her best and perhaps she would gain access to the power she had demonstrated before.

We would need to resolve this quickly if we were going to join Arabella before her fight with Samson was concluded.

Hong Tao's fighting skills were formidable, and he showed no obvious signs of magic use. I was surprised he had managed to hold the five of us off this long.

That was not to say Hong Tao was unscathed. His body was bruised, battered, and his breathing came in heavy pants.

His compatriot Olympia had used the *imperi* and teleported elsewhere and Samson was making his way to the *Tinosa* leaving Hong Tao alone.

Not only was Hong Tao holding us off, he had incapacitated Frey and Freya quite quickly. I did not know how much training they had received to begin with so it may not have been an impressive feat.

They had Berserker names, but it was clear they were no Berserkers. Berserker children were trained from birth to be fighters and I wondered why their mother had chosen such names for the twins.

Regardless of their skill, Hong Tao had also managed to evade us and Lady Gorin's *yandhi* until the spell had ended and the *yandhi* had dematerialized.

I knew little of dwarven magics, but I knew of the fire constructs that some of them had been able to create. It was how they had been so efficient at repelling the invasions of the Sitkin Berserkers throughout the previous eras.

I had been surprised to see the dwarven lady after she had put us to sleep and refused to help us. It was a good surprise.

After all, it was thanks to her that my previous injuries had been healed. I owed her a debt that I did not know how to repay.

It was now two versus one as Lady Gorin and Lancer Solace fought him together. Hong Tao's proficiency made me wonder just how capable the leader of the First Constellation Jesuit was.

Hong Tao and Samson shared the same rank but there was such a large gap in power that I wondered how we could win in a fight against Jesuit, even as a squad.

We would need backup and although Lancer Solace had sent several pigeons requesting assistance when they came they would go to Fort Mudo or Opulake.

There was no way for them to find us here in Jormondor and if Jesuit came here for the *imperi* himself I was not too optimistic about our chances.

It was only a matter of time before Hong Tao fell to our combined force but the sooner the better. I just did not know how to bring that about.

While the twins were out cold Hua stood in between the fighting and the injured frozen in place as her eyes darted from Frey to her father. I had not seen her hesitate before now and it worried me.

I wondered if her determination had faltered. In the face of actually killing her father perhaps her loyalty would shift and that was the last thing we needed right now.

I hurried over to where she stood. If she could help Lancer Solace and Lady Gorin while I healed the twins it would be very helpful or vice versa.

I grabbed her by the shoulders and locked eyes with her. I could see the fear and doubt in her eyes, and I knew she needed a call to action.

"Hua, we don't know each other very well, but remember why you are here," I said. "We are here to defeat Hong Tao, your father. I will take care of Frey and Freya. Your father is right there. Be the onryō you said you were," I said.

She nodded slowly and after glancing at Frey once more she placed her hand on my shoulder.

"Thank you, Pershing Micah. Do not let Frey die and I will do the opposite for my father, how about that?" Hua said.

I smiled and nodded and then Hua turned and went to join Lancer Solace and Lady Gorin while I hurried towards Frey and Freya.

Unlike Arabella they were close by. I could give them quick first aid and then return to the fight with Hong Tao.

I was out of magic, but I still had a second piece of whey. I left it in the black wrapper like we had when I was a recruit and ate it.

It tasted of sweet chicken on buttery rice all at once. I swallowed the entire serving and felt magic streaming through my body as my fatigue faded.

I had magic now, but I lack the talent to heal their injuries as they needed. I did not let this discourage me as I could still help with my first aid kit too.

Frey looked the worst, so I decided to focus on him. I glanced back and saw Lancer Solace engaging with Hong Tao in close combat while Lady Gorin aimed bolts of fire at him.

I managed to heal Frey's broken wrist and quickly healed a large purple bruise that reached around his neck. The purple receded into a point of nothingness. The bandage around his hell hound bite was bleeding again so I took off the old bandaging.

He had just been brought back to life. I did not think Arabella would be able repeat the feat. We would not lose him again.

Around the wound was black ooze that made me wrinkle my nose from the smell. I wiped it away and wrapped another bandage around it.

I was not sure what to do about the black ooze. Surely it was from the type of bite, but I did not have the insight to care for it properly.

I checked his pulse and although he remained unconscious his pulse was steady, so I turned my attention to his sister next.

Freya had a matching purple bruise on the right side of her face and both her eyes were swollen shut. Her breathing was quick and from the temperature of her forehead she had a fever.

"Frigga," Freya murmured through her fever, and I wondered who that was and unless I was mistaken it sounded like another Berserker name.

I could heal Freya's basic wounds but if there was something deeper that was ailing her, I wouldn't be able to cure it. I was glad that I only saw bruises. They were easier to heal than bone breaks and deep cuts.

I managed to heal her wounds and although it was a very slow process, when it was done, I still had a decent amount of magic left.

I might have been the only one left with magic. It seemed Savant had used the rest of his magic stalling for me because when I had last looked he was not Channeling.

I had assumed much of Lady Gorin's magic was invested in the dragon of fire and that when it dispersed, she had run out, but she had continued to aim fireballs at Hong Tao for an additional minute or so.

That had subsided now, and she had moved forward and joined the hand to hand fight with Lancer Solace.

I grabbed the wrist of each twin and pulled them away until they were safely out of the range of the fight and away from the globs of steaming fire that littered the cavern ground after they had dripped down from the dragon of flames.

Just as I was going to turn and join the others I saw blood leaking from the back of Freya's head and realized I had missed an injury.

I frowned in frustration. If I had been more proficient with healing I would have been able to feel the injury when I had healed her previously.

I knelt and carefully lifted her head so that I could see better and saw a wound that left her hair sticky with blood.

Gingerly I parted her orange hair. It looked like when she had been incapacitated she had fallen and hit a rock or something and that was the cause of the bleeding.

I healed what I could of the injury, separated her hair as best as I could, and placed a bandage on the wound from my first aid kit.

After I was done with Freya I remembered my promise to Hua that I would not let Frey die and just to be safe I quickly double checked him for any injuries that I might have missed but there were none.

With the twins settled I let out a sigh of relief and ran over to where the others fought Hong Tao. Remaining farther back than the others I took stock of the situation.

I wanted to see where I could assist best and did not want to disrupt the flow of battle for my allies. Lancer Solace outstretched his hand and using his aura he constructed a set of chains and attached them into the ground. I was glad to see he was not out of magic, but instead had been waiting for my arrival.

Hua pulled out an orb filled with a green liquid and threw it at Hong Tao. The chains prevented him from moving and the glass cracked against his skin causing the green liquid to drip down his chest.

She withdrew another orb but the second one looked empty and threw it at Hong Tao. As it burst it let out an almighty boom of sound throughout the cavern and a large crack formed on the ceiling above us.

Hong Tao groaned and fell to his knees and would have been pierced by a falling stalactite if I had not sent a burst of my aura to throw it off.

There were puddles of water just behind Hong Tao. If he could just move back a bit, I could immobilize him with Berserker magic, and we could cuff him and take him in alive.

I had suffered several blows to my ego recently. Hong Tao had decimated me on the beach. The etsans had restrained me in their webs and drained all my magic and Lady Gorin had knocked me unconscious quite easily.

Although she didn't, Lady Gorin could have killed Arabella and I then and there and the same could be said about the First Constellation leaders when they had defeated us on the beach.

I could not afford to lose anymore, and I would make them regret leaving us alive.

I liked how Hong Tao did not banter like Olympia and Samson. He simply fought silently and did not speak to any of us, not even Hua.

Lady Gorin reached to wrap her arm around Hong Tao's neck but before she could Hong Tao gritted his teeth and broke the aura chains that restrained him.

As I wondered how he was so strong, Hong Tao elbowed Lady Gorin in the gut and tore his green stained shirt off.

Lancer Solace caught my eye and with a twitch of his fingers I knew which maneuver he wanted us to do. We were on the same wavelength, and I began to summon my magic.

I exhaled deeply and my breath was pale white and visible. I felt goosebumps rise across my body along with a chill that accompanied the sensation.

I raised both my hands and aimed my index fingers with my thumbs up at Hong Tao's feet. The maneuver Lancer Solace had picked required my patience and precision, so I waited for my moment.

Lancer Solace managed to slam his aura enhanced fist into Hong Tao's chest with amazing force causing Hong Tao to let out a groan of pain and stagger backwards.

Lady Gorin watched me carefully, not wanting to interfere in our scheme. She was an intelligent woman and I wondered what she would do after we had defeated the First Constellation.

The stagger of Hong Tao had caused his feet to shift and the second his right foot landed in the puddle of water I exhaled deeply, exhaled a ghostly white breath, and commanded the water to freeze.

The liquid obeyed and with a snap of the fingers of my right hand the water froze and encased Hong Tao's foot in ice.

The maneuver threw him more off balance but, while he was unsteady, Lady Gorin wrapped her arms around Hong Tao's torso and held him tight leaving his arms pinned to his sides.

Hong Tao struggled and bulged. With a grunt he broke Lady Gorin's embrace and elbowed her in the jaw. He lifted his foot and broke the ice that had restrained him.

Lady Gorin spit out a glob of blood but did not hesitate to quickly attempt to grapple Hong Tao once more, but he dunked her arms.

I watched his feet closely, waiting for his feet to touch the puddles once more, but it seemed he went out of his way to avoid the water.

"I guess that trick only works once," I muttered and rushed forward.

Savant grasped Hong Tao by his sides and with a grunt his wine colored aura flared to life filling the air with scents of chocolate. Savant lifted Hong Tao into the air and with a spin he kicked Hong Tao to the right, and he flew back narrowly avoiding Lady Gorin.

Hua, who had also been watching and waiting leapt forward, straddled Hong Tao, and forced his wrists onto the ground.

Hong Tao looked at her like she was a stranger. I did not see a hint of love in his eyes, and I wondered how a father and child could be so distant.

My thoughts turned to my own father who had been my biggest supporter when he had been alive. He would have even encouraged me to join the Mystio even though I was his only son if that was what I wanted to do.

It seemed everyone was not so lucky.

"Father," Hua pleaded. "Mother is gone, don't you know you can't bring her back?"

Hong Tao gritted his teeth in response, and I saw something shift in his eyes, but he did not speak, and I was left to wonder about Hong Tao's intentions.

Hong Tao tensed and before we could react he lifted his legs and kneed Hua from behind causing her to lose her grip on Hong Tao's wrists.

With his wrists free he slapped Hua in the face and threw her off of him. He began to rise but Savant and I wrapped him in a harness of bordeaux and green aura and pinned him to the ground.

I rushed over and helped Hua to her feet. She glared at Hong Tao sadly.

"Mother would hate that you're working with the First Constellation. You know what they're doing now is not what great grandfather envisioned, don't you?"

Hong Tao closed his eyes and attempted to break his restraints and although it cracked, I was quickly able to reinforce it.

I was not sure how he was so strong. His strength was not beyond belief, but it was on the edge of human comprehension.

I pulled out the yellow cuffs Hong Tao had used on us on the beach and swung them in front of him.

"Remember these?" I asked.

I knelt in front of him and eased the aura construct up so that I could clasp the cuffs around Hong Tao's wrists. If his strength was magical hopefully the cuffs would reduce it.

I would have preferred to have cuffed him with his wrists behind him but that was not possible with the angle he lay at, so his wrists were cuffed at the front.

Savant and I slowly reduced our aura and lifted Hong Tao onto his feet. Hong Tao sagged in a defeated manner, but I was on guard for a ploy.

After allowing Samson to escape in Opulake I was not interested in allowing any of the other bandits to escape. The destruction of the bandit group was one of my mother's main focuses and for once we had the same goal.

With Hong Tao restrained I looked towards where Arabella had been and began to make my way over to help.

Something glinted out of the corner of my eye and I saw a magnificent dagger with a red gem on its hilt. I grabbed it, deciding to study it later, and turned my attention back to Arabella.

I saw Samson in the water swimming towards the *Tinosa* but there was no sign of Arabella. Could she be in the water?

Before I could reach her, the cavern groaned and shook. I paused and looked upwards, and I saw the crack caused by Hua's orb begin to spread, and then a downpour of huge rocks crashed onto the cavern floor and formed a wall to the ceiling that blocked my path and sight to Arabella.

As they slammed onto the ground the force of them threw off my balance and I fell back.

"No!" I said in frustration. "Arabella!" I yelled.

I slammed my aura coated fist into the rock, but it remained in place. The others came over to assist. Lancer Solace attempted to move the rocks, but they did not budge.

Hua took several glass bulbs from her bag and threw them at the rocks. The rocks melted slightly but overall, there was no change.

"These rocks are old, they will not move," Lady Gorin said sadly.

I glanced at Lady Gorin and Hua. We might not have defeated Hong Tao if not for their assistance. I was grateful for their help, but I felt hopeless over Arabella's situation.

"Thank you for your help, Lady Gorin," Lancer Solace said as he grasped Lady Gorin's forearm tightly, "and Hua," he said as he repeated the thank you gesture with her.

Lady Gorin nodded and said, "But the human woman got away with the *imperi*. It seems I have finally failed my assignment."

"We will do our best to apprehend her, and if possible, return the *imperi* to your custody," Lancer Solace said.

That was definitely not protocol. My mother wouldn't like his call at all, but then again, she wouldn't be hearing about it from me.

"What's going to happen to my father?" Hua asked. "Are they going to burn him?"

"It is up to the Queen and the Dog Court," Lancer Solace said, but we both knew with a case like this the Dog Court was more for show and that Hong Tao as a First Constellation lieutenant would most definitely be used as an example.

Hua nodded as if she already knew this, and I wondered how satisfied she was with not killing him herself.

"I can take Frey and Freya with the *imperi* we have. I entrust you with my father. May he see my mother's face once more," she said not looking at her father.

"Let me see this *imperi* you speak of," Lady Gorin said.

Hua pulled out the shimmering gem of black and rainbows and after hesitating a second, she transferred it to Lady Gorin.

At her touch the *imperi* seemed to glow even brighter and after a second of study Lady Gorin nodded her head.

"It is indeed an *imperi,* but its magic is fading. It will not have enough energy to carry three people a long distance, two at the most, and after this jump its magic will be gone completely."

Hua shook her head quickly. She dabbed a line of the black ooze from Frey's lips and frowned deeply.

"Frey needs help, a real doctor. I will take him back to South Dresden where his family lives. Can you take care of his sister until she can join us?"

I knew the protective Freya would not like being separated from her brother, but the civilians were out of our control as long as they did not interfere with our mission.

My mother would have wanted the *imperi* but if Lady Gorin was correct and it had only a small amount of magic, I did not see the harm in letting Hua use it to get Frey to a doctor.

After all, Lady Gorin had said that it had only been enough for one more trip anyways; soon it would be nothing more than a pretty stone. I had promised he would not die and chances would be better if he could meet with an actual doctor.

Ultimately everything was Lancer Solace's call and I looked towards him for his verdict on the situation. He was silent for a moment. Lancer Solace always took his time before speaking.

"We must make our way to Jemny, and we will take the eastern route which will go through South Dresden. We will tend to Freya until she wakes and if she wishes she may travel with us.

"Thank you, Lancer Solace and Pershing-" she began but halted as she realized she did not know my last name.

"Zhang," I finished and as the name rang a bell in Hua's head her eyes widened but she did not speak on it. After all we had been through I felt comfortable giving my true last name.

"Thank you, Pershing Zhang," she said then walked away from us and her father without another word and towards Frey and his sister.

Hua checked Freya's injuries. After doing so she placed her hand on Frey's and a glowing sphere of dark purple magic spiraled growing larger until it blocked them from my view and once it faded, they were gone leaving only Freya behind.

"What are you going to do now?" I asked Lady Gorin.

"I shall stay here. This is my home," she said with a smile.

"B-but the *imperi* is gone. Won't you be alone here?" I asked in surprise.

I did not know what I thought she would do but it was not that she would remain in Jormondor alone. Especially after the death of her metal golem that had been her only companion.

"If my kin call for me, I will answer but until then I will guard the great city of Jormondor," Lady Gorin said.

"Is there a way to get to the surface from here? We can try to reach Arabella from the surface," Lancer Solace said, and Lady Gorin nodded.

"We can use the Tower of Oqubay," she said with a frown. "The Tower of Oqubay can get you to the surface but it will not be as close to here as you wish," she said.

"How close?" Lancer Solace asked, and Lady Gorin's answer left me feeling hopeless.

Arabella would be on her own.

Chapter
SEVENTEEN

oqubay

"Was that a dog made of metal I saw?" Lancer Solace asked as we made our way through the tunnel back towards the Tower of Oqubay.

Lady Gorin nodded.

"Aye, his name was Canis," Lady Gorin said sadly. "We dwarves craft our golems once we reach adulthood. I chose the form of a dog for Canis, and we had been bonded for over one hundred years."

I could hear the pain in her voice though she shed no tears. I had never been a big fan of dogs but I knew

Lancer Solace had two dogs at our base in Zaebos so he would be more empathetic of her loss.

To me animals were animals, but my mother was also a big fan of dogs, hence the Dog Court. They often roamed the Eternal Palace with each animal having their own dedicated handler.

The dogs always panted heavily as if they were dehydrated, and I always said it was because they belonged in Sitka.

The capital city of Jemny was in the northern parts of the kingdom and was cold enough during the winters but during the summer the city was at the mercy of Astria and Zaniah.

"I have seen and studied the golems but not one that was still operational. I am sorry you lost him assisting us," Lancer Solace said, and I could hear the apology in his tone.

"But it was made of metal? Can it not be repaired?" I asked.

Canis had been torn in half somehow but both pieces in his body had been intact from what I had seen, and I wondered if he could be mended someway since he was mechanical not organic.

Lady Gorin shifted Freya on her shoulder, for she had insisted she carry her before replying.

"Once, perhaps, but no longer. We had several Life Crafters, the greatest being Risotto Steelkiss, but they were all killed by humans during the Battle of Minato."

I expected to hear bitterness in her voice, but she spoke evenly.

"How did this city survive the tsunami?" I asked Lady Gorin. The question had been in the back of my mind since we had arrived.

"When the wave came, the guards of the *imperi* here used the Tower of Oqubay to bring the city here," she replied.

"The whole city?" Lancer Solace asked, surprise in his voice and Lady Gorin nodded. "How do these towers work?"

"The past is done, there is no reason to dwell on it. The Age of the *Nani* is over. Killing the lot of you, even you Berserker, would not heal my non beating heart. It would not bring back those I have lost," she said to me.

"I understand that, but it does not mean you have to help us further," I said. "An alliance against the First Constellation I understood but they are gone now," I said.

Lady Gorin shrugged.

"Humans are humans," she said. "This will give me something to do before I return to my isolation."

"So, you will not come with us?" Lancer Solace asked. "I could guarantee your safety."

"You could not," Lady Gorin replied, and she did not speak further.

Our pace was not as quick as I would have liked. Our injuries slowed us, and we also had to transport the restrained Hong Tao. It all stalled our reunion with Arabella and Samson.

We finally arrived at the edge of the city, and I was glad to see my ice bridge was still intact. I found myself grateful that I had not broken it down but the sight of it only made me think more of Arabella and I gritted my teeth in frustration.

How could I have let her get separated? I should have insisted on staying with her. Those had been my orders.

"Berserker magic," Lady Gorin said and stepped onto the ice slide with no hesitation.

"You know of it?" I asked and carefully stepped onto the ice slide.

"We had repelled the Berserker clans for hundreds of years. Southern humans defeated us and then the Berserkers conquered them and now they rule this land."

Berserkers were human too, but they had mostly lived in Sitka, the frozen lands north of Damasyr but after my father had defeated King Nairobi many Berserkers had migrated south into Damasyr.

Going upwards on the ice slide was much slower than going down it had been, especially with Hong Tao with us.

Although he did not resist and kept up with us as he returned to Jormondor he was forced to move with my arm on his and with his hands cuffed, which slowed us further.

Despite the hurdles I surmised that it was still far quicker than traversing through the city streets below.

Once we reached the top of the tower I glanced at where the *imperi* had once been held and I thought of Arabella once more.

She had been the one to free the *imperi*. She would be able to defeat Samson. I had to have faith.

"I will activate the Tower of Okubay and get you to the Tower of Arkebay. Time moves differently when we use the towers, but it will get you to the surface. I only ask that you not tell others of the city. I know one day humans will find this city again as they have before. I also know that the humans who took the *imperi* from here may spread the word but the longer this city can remain sacred the better."

I wondered how the Tower of Oqubay would get us to the eastern coast as Lady Gorin had said and what she meant by time moving differently but I was so tired I could tell no jokes nor ask any questions.

Lancer Solace hesitated before speaking. Leaving out information like this in a report to the Queen could get him in trouble with the Queen and his father.

"Thank you for your assistance," he said after a moment. "I can not speak for others, but I will not tell of Jormondor.

I looked across the city of Jormondor. It was a magnificent city. There were only one or two human cities in Damasyr that could match its vast scale.

And it was empty.

I wondered if humans could rekindle the city. Some creatures would have to be removed for safety, but it seemed a sad shame that something so great was hidden underground forgotten.

Then I looked at Lady Gorin and thought of her loss. She was alone and had nothing left. She was helping us at no cost to us and all she wanted was the solitude that was draped across the great city.

I swallowed and said, "I will do the same."

Lady Gorin nodded and leaned forward to shift Freya into our arms. She then turned and walked over to a bowl on the tower floor and after fumbling with it for a bit she was able to reattach it properly to its base.

As Lady Gorin worked I noticed an orb glowing with etches of light. It was a communication orb. My mother had one in the royal vault. They had been used by the dwarves to send messages over long distances and my mother had been trying to use them for years.

But this one had a message.

Before I could ask Lady Gorin about it the pedestal was reassembled. Lady Gorin closed her eyes and pricked her finger on a jagged part of the pedestal.

Several drops of blood streamed down the bowl and suddenly the tower began to vibrate like I had felt before while we fought the fire lizards.

The world shifted and I was forced to blink. When I opened my eyes once more, we were in a world of fire.

I coughed harshly as the heat grabbed at me and I fell onto my knees letting go of my grip on Freya. I heard the echoes of voices in pain emanating from all around us and covered my ears.

I looked down from the Tower of Oqubay and saw rivers of lava and black rock like obsidian across the ground instead of dirt and grass.

Arabella and the Tower of Magic

In the sky I saw a winged creature soaring towards the Tower of Oqubay and I forced myself onto my feet in preparation.

"The Tower's calibration is off!" Lady Gorin yelled. "I need you to stall!"

She turned around and began to fiddle with the base of the pedestal trusting us to guard her while she worked.

I gritted my teeth and exhaled deeply. Lancer Solace laid Freya onto the tower floor, and she stirred but did not wake.

As the winged creature loomed closer, I saw that the winged creature was actually a man. Well, he was a man with large leathery black wings. Above his head were two horns that appeared to be made of blood that dripped onto his head, but he did not seem bothered by it.

He wore nothing but an orange loincloth with a very muscular body and black eyes that reminded me of Savant's dark eyes.

I saw something twitch behind him and saw that he had a tail like a lizard, but it was sharp and pointed like the head of an arrowhead.

The winged man snarled something in a language I did not understand and without turning to face him Lady Gorin said something back in the same language to the man.

The flying figure spat, and I stepped backwards as he spit towards us, and his spittle caused steam to rise from the tower floor as it made contact.

"Incoming! Fiend!" Lady Gorin called.

In his hands the winged man conjured a wand of black stone traced throughout it with fiery marks that glowed and shimmered.

I lifted my hand and constructed a short green spear made of aura and launched it towards the fiend, but he dodged and pointed the wand at us in response.

I dived to the side hoping to avoid whatever his attack was. Around us four dark purple portals appeared on the tower floor and out of them rotting figures began to crawl out of them.

I spotted a woman with long dirty black hair with a large hole in her stomach that revealed her organs. The woman's eyes burned like fire, and she clawed out of the portal and onto the tower floor.

"Ghouls!" Lady Gorin yelled over the groaning and mumbling of the creatures.

I had heard of ghouls but never met one. The sorcerers of Z'etoile often used them as servants. They were dead and unfeeling, and their creation was forbidden in Damasyr, Cypress, *and* Sitka.

"Use these and do not let the ghouls touch or bite you," Lady Gorin said as she threw something that glowed blue towards Savant and I.

I caught it and inspected what she had thrown to me. It was a gemstone and I saw that it was in fact not glowing and had just caught the light when it was in the air.

I identified the stone as azurite. It was a deep blue mineral shaped with six sides that were tipped at both ends.

I did not know of the correlation between azurite and ghouls, but I gripped it tightly and glanced towards Lancer Solace.

Next to Lancer Solace from a second portal I recognized the Mystio Eufaula O'Conner. She looked at me blankly and my heart experienced a pang of pain at the sight of her.

Her uniform was in tatters, and she was missing her boots. Her Mystio chest piece was broken in halves and hung uselessly from her shoulders.

Her eyes glowed pink and I heard Lancer Solace call her name. The emotion in his voice made my eyes water.

I had not been very close to Eufaula, but I had met her several times and knew how close she and Lancer Solace had been. Her death had taken a large toll on him and the effects of it were still ongoing.

It was cruel for him to be exposed to her in this manner and I figured that the woman next to Lady Gorin was her partner, Lady Kuri.

Even Freya had a portal of her own and out of the portal had emerged a girl that looked just like her. I would have called them twins if she had not already had one. Perhaps they had once been triplets.

"Uncuff me," Hong Tao demanded, speaking for the first time in quite a while.

Behind him a portal had opened and out of it a woman who looked like an older Hua was coming out of it. I figured it had to be Hua's mother and Hong Tao's significant other.

With my forehead dripping with sweat I rushed forward and pulled Freya away from the ghoul that had been leaning towards her.

Each portal had produced someone important to us and I could not focus on Hua's mother for long as I began to get a sinking feeling.

Lady Kuri for Lady Gorin, Eufaula for Lancer Solace, and it seemed the girl out of Freya's portal was also someone she was familiar with.

That left only me.

I turned to the right and saw him.

He appeared as I had last seen him with the stance and attire befitting the status of a king. He and I had always looked so very similar to the chagrin of my mother, although he had always kept his hair longer than I.

He wore black boots and pants that were tucked as we Mystio did. His top was a dark purple with gold buttons and lining at the hem. A white belt with gold accents was latched on top of the shirt and near his left shoulder the sigil of a white polar bear sat pinning his white quarter cape.

Always was in his dress clothes I thought, feeling my eyes growing warmer.

The tears rolled down my cheeks as I smiled sadly at him and then bowed slightly as he had taught me.

"I am king, Aiguo," he had said, his deep voice rumbling in my ears even now. "We must respect custom and tradition. In public I am King Ambrocio, and you are Prince Aiguo.

I swallowed and finally found my voice.

"Long time no see, Your Highness," I managed with a slight smile. "How have you been, Father?"

Chapter EIGHTEEN

ambrocio

"King Ambrocio is dead, my Queen," the Ranger Commander had said.

The streets had been overflowing with Damasyri lords, nobles, and warriors. My father had left for Cypress months prior and the whole of Jemny was present awaiting his return.

His banners had been reported throughout the kingdom and we had expected he and his entourage to return that day.

Yet leading the entourage was the Ranger Commander Hermes instead of my father the king. The Ranger Commander had dismounted his pony and with his head bowed he slowly approached my mother.

The Rangers treated their ponies like humans. Rangers explored Damasyr and even other countries and their horses took them wherever they needed to go.

Hermes's pony, El Tibo, was filthy. El Tibo lowered its head and began to drink thirstily from a puddle in the street.

Ranger Commander Hermes knelt onto his knee with his head lowered as he waited for my mother to speak. In Damasyr the person of higher rank began important conversations such as this and my family had continued the custom.

I broke rank from where I had been standing and rushed towards Hermes. As I moved, I felt the hands of Adela, my mentor reach for me.

I managed to duck her grip and I placed my hand on Hermes's shoulder and shook it. After all, this had to be one of his jokes, he always told the worst jokes, and everyone knew it.

"Prince Aiguo!" I heard her hiss, but I ignored her.

Ranger Commander Hermes had been one of my father's consultants and they were even close friends along with Mysteif Biawatcheeitchish, who was the leader of the Mystio.

Many simply called her Mysteif Bia but my father had always insisted I address her by her full name yet in that moment all decorum vanished.

I buried my face into Hermes's chest and hugged him tightly. I knew all of Jemny was watching but I did not care.

"Hermes, where is my father?" I cried. "Where is Bia? Where are Marva, Serrono and Sly? Hermes!"

Hermes kept his head lowered and ignored me and it was only seconds before I felt arms grab me and pull me away and back into formation.

I glanced towards my mother but saw only distaste for me on her face. Her expression hurt my feelings. It seemed she was always so disappointed in me.

"What happened to my King Husband?" my mother said, all traces of emotion gone from her face. She was regal and stone.

"We were at sea with President Chisam, General Secretary Priyank, and Genghis Jarl, and of Baluga of Padawan. The leaders had met to discuss a worldwide truce and alliance and were discussing terms while hunting sea snakes. A fearsome storm brewed, and the ship went down. The *Sea Giant* went down and only President Chisam was found."

Hermes's words echoed in my ears. It couldn't be true. My father had gripped my hand before leaving. He had *promised* he'd be back by my birthday which had been a week prior.

I had been planning to tease him for his tardiness but now I would never see him again.

"And where were you, Ranger Commander," my mother had asked and even though I didn't think it was possible his head was lowered even further.

"Genghis Jarl insisted on the privacy of their meeting and the King conceded. I had no choice in the matter," Hermes said.

"Well," my mother said and then bit her lip hard before standing. "It seemed we have no use for you any longer, Hermes. Leave your cape, bow, and emblem here and leave this city. Return when you have found my husband."

"As you have decreed, my queen," Hermes said. He stood slowly not meeting my or anyone else's eyes. He unclipped his cape and laid it along with his bow on the ground in front of my mother.

"If I may, my queen," he said, and she nodded.

Hermes strode over to me and knelt onto one knee in front of me.

"My prince— or should I say my king," Hermes began but I had cut him off.

"I don't want you to go," I had said but Hermes continued onwards as if he had not heard me.

"Stay strong," Hermes said. "If your father is alive, I will find him and if he no longer draws breath then as his protector I have no right to be in your sight."

"But Hermes—" I started but my friend had simply placed the scissor-tailed flycatcher emblem in my hand. The green metal glistened and was cold in my hand.

Hermes said no more as he stood and walked away. The procession parted for him to pass, and it seemed that all Damasyr began to jeer and boo at Hermes.

I stepped after him but was grasped successfully this time by Adela. My heart throbbed. Even if my father was dead Hermes did not deserve to be disparaged like this. He had saved my father's life twice while he had been his bodyguard.

"Hermes!" I called but he didn't look back. "I don't want to be king!"

"No worries, Augio," my mother said. "You will not be king for some time."

I looked at her and she was smiling.

Shaking my head to remove it of the memories, I stared at my father. He had not answered my question, but I had not really expected him to.

I exhaled deeply through my nostrils and held the azurite up between the ghoul and I. Hong Tao struggled against his bounds, but I ignored him, and kicked at Freya mildly hoping to wake her from her slumber.

Three ghouls were pressing in, and I was against the ledge of the Tower of Oqubay. When I shifted my hand from ghoul to ghoul one would freeze and recoil, but the others would attempt to close the distance.

It was only a matter of time before they overwhelmed me, so I made the executive decision to release Hong Tao from his cuffs and shook Freya with my free hand.

I heard her mumble something but could not afford to look away from the ghouls. Over their shoulders I saw Lancer Solace battling both the ghoul of Eufaula, the ghoul of who I had presumed was Lady Kuri, and the winged man while Lady Gorin tinkered with the tower pedestal.

"Know anything about ghouls?" I asked Hong Tao and he nodded.

"They are weak to fire, and don't let them kill you. If you die, they can turn you into a ghoul also. Their bite and claws are deadly, avoid them piercing your skin at any cost," he said, his eyes on the ghoul woman the whole time.

Once again, I wished Adonis had been on this mission. He knew words of power that could summon dwarven fire. My ice would be no use here.

"Great," I said. "None of us can use fire magic."

I was tired and both my magic reserves were low. The ice bridge had exhausted almost all of my ice magic and my aura reserve was just a little bit above my ice magic.

Freya began rising from the tower floor. She rubbed her eyes and I saw them focus on the ghoul girl approaching us.

"Frigga?" she whispered and took a step towards the ghoul. She would have continued further if I had not stopped her with my arm.

"She's not real," I told Freya and she looked from me to Hong Tao next to me. "It's not her."

"How long was I out? What is *he* doing here? Where's my brother?" she asked looking around the tower floor for him.

A roar of magma burst from the ground nearby and Freya stumbled away from the edge of the tower ledge.

"Are we dead?" she asked.

"Not yet!" I said glancing at the ghouls and the winged man.

We had no fire, but we were surrounded by fire. A simple plan began to formulate in my head, and I explained it to Hong Tao and Freya.

"You trust him?" Freya whispered. "Last thing I remembered him doing was throwing Frey's body at me and then I woke up here. Also, you never said where my brother is."

"After," I promised. "And we have no choice but to take his assistance. There are too many variables."

Freya looked like she wanted to say more but instead she just nodded, and I handed her the azurite. She slid it in her pocket and once it was out of sight the ghoul rushed towards us.

They were faster than they looked, and it was little over a second before they were on us. Freya whimpered as the ghoul of Frigga came first while the other two snarled but did not approach us.

Freya dropped onto her back avoiding the ghoul's arms and while it was busy with her, I turned and grabbed the ghoul's waist and tossed it over the side of the tower.

It howled as it fell but went quiet once it fell into a stream of lava. Freya remained whimpering on the ground, and I extended my arm to help her up.

"I'm sorry, but it wasn't her," I said, trying to convince us both but before I could lift her, I felt the arms of a ghoul wrap around me. I saw the velvet sleeve and knew which ghoul it was.

"Father, please," I cried as I struggled.

It was stronger than I and as I tried to break its grip it tightened its arms around me, pinning my arms to my side, restricting my movement.

Freya rose off the ground, calling my name, and pulled out the whip she used for combat. She rolled backwards, aimed, and snapped the whip at the ghoul of my father.

The whip wrapped around the head of the ghoul and began to sizzle where the whip made contact with its skin. Freya tightened her grip, pulled, and after a wet sick ripping sound, the ghoul of my father lost its head, and I cringed as I heard the head hit the ground.

Despite its decapitation the ghoul kept its grip on me, and it was not until Hong Tao broke the ghoul's grip on me by punching its elbows and then prying its arms open.

"Quickly, all of him into the lava," he shouted and then turned his attention to the ghoul of the woman. It rushed towards him. "Where is the azurite?" he asked.

"Freya!" I called and after a moment of hesitation Freya pulled the azurite from her pocket and tossed it to Hong Tao.

Hong Tao held it up and the ghoul froze. I looked away and grabbed the arms of the ghoul of my father. It was hard not to think of the ghoul as my father and mentally I apologized.

The hands were just as my father's had been. They held the same scars and lines. The fingers reached towards my skin, as I threw the headless body from the tower. I looked away quickly, afraid to watch them fall.

"The head too?" Freya asked and I looked over to see Freya holding my father's head carefully.

"Your father was the king?" Freya asked me, staring at the head and I nodded, not trusting myself to speak.

It felt as if I had lost my father all over again, but it was worse this time as I had held on to the hope that Hermes would find him and bring him home the first time, but now there was no hope. If he was a ghoul, he was probably dead.

"Mine was my sister," she said. "You helped me, let me help you."

Before I regained my ability to speak and before I could say goodbye, she threw the ghoul's head into the lava leaving only the last woman ghoul.

With only one of them left it was easier to catch it and between the three of us we managed to get her to the edge of the tower. Just as we were able to send her into the lava, Hong Tao halted us.

He held the azurite in the air and glanced at us. He could leave us to the mercy of the ghoul without the azurite and I immediately regretted my decision to trust him.

After all, the word of a bandit only mattered if you had a sharper knife than them and I currently had none but my throwing knives.

I was calculating whether I could reach a throwing knife and disarm him when Hong Tao lowered the azurite and threw the azurite to me.

"I will go with my wife," he said as I caught the azurite.

Although my mother would want him brought in alive, I did not stop him as he approached the ghoul of his wife. He would have been sentenced to death anyways and I believed that was the right verdict as a leader of the First Constellation.

If I managed to stop him and bring him to Jemny my mother would only make an event of his death, something I didn't agree with.

"It's not her," I whispered, and Hong Tao smiled to my surprise.

"Of course, it isn't," he said. "But she is all I was after. I was going to use the *imperi* to find a world where she still lived but here she is here."

Hong Tao gripped the ghoul's hand, and it bit him hard in the shoulder. He pulled her to the edge and then hesitated.

"Please tell Hua," he started then shook his head and I saw tears leap from his eyes. "Forget it, she remembers," he said and without another word he jumped off pulling the ghoul with him.

I rushed to the edge and glanced over the side, but their bodies were already gone except for two burning hands interlocked above the lava until they had sunk too, leaving no evidence that Hong Tao had ever existed.

I wiped tears from my cheeks and saw Freya mimic the gesture. It seemed in the end that Hong Tao really did care about Hua despite how he had acted previously.

"Come on, let's help the others," I said but Freya did not move.

"Where is my brother?" she asked, and I glanced at Lancer Solace. The ghouls were gone but he was still battling the winged man.

I knew he had to be exhausted after our battle with   Hong Tao and he needed backup immediately.

"Your brother is alive, Hua used an *imperi* to take him to South Dresden for a doctor," I said quickly.

"He left me?" she whispered, her voice thick with betrayal.

"There was not enough magic for all of you. It was Hua's call, more details later, I promise."

I rushed towards Lady Gorin just as a flash of light burst from the pedestal.

"It's ready," she said. "We just need to get that demon out of our air space; otherwise, he'll be brought along with us, and trust me, you don't want that."

I nodded and looked at Lancer Solace and caught his eye. I held up two fingers, so he knew which maneuver I was attempting.

Lancer Solace nodded his head slowly and I exhaled deeply. I pressed my hands together and felt a chill in my palms.

As I separated my hands a pole of ice emerged. I stretched my arms as far as they could go and then caught the rod of ice.

A chill spread from my lungs and I gasped as I felt the weight of the spell. I did not think I would not be able to use my Berserker magic for some time.

Using my aura, I sharpened the ice into a makeshift spear and gripped it tightly. I watched as Lancer Solace began the maneuver.

He used his aura to propel himself in the air. His sudden elevation seemed to catch the demon off guard and before the demon could recover Lancer Solace Channeled a large mallet made of bordeaux energy and slammed it into the demon's chest.

The demon slammed into the tower floor with a sick *crack* coming from its right wing. As it began to rise, I rushed forward. I remembered the dagger I had found so I tossed the ice spear and pulled out the dagger.

The demon ducked the spear as I knew it would and the spear clattered against the wall behind the demon and rolled to a stop by its feet.

As the demon had paused to dodge the spear I leaned in and stabbed the dagger into the demon's chest where I thought its heart would be.

I was very low on magic for the maneuver I had chosen and had to improvise. I pulled the spear of ice into my hand, slammed it into the demon's gut, and planted it on the ground. With a burst of my Berserker magic, I extended the spear driving the pierced demon upwards.

Lancer Solace repeated his move that drove him into the air and once more Channeling a large mallet he swung it into the demon breaking the ice and sending him over the edge of the tower.

"Brace yourself," I heard Lady Gorin yell, but I had no time to brace anything as the Tower of Oqubay began to vibrate and we were teleported out of the world of fire and onto a beach.

I looked to the sky and sighed in relief.

Two suns.

PART THREE

Arabella of Opulake, The Prophet of Eloah

Chapter NINETEEN

estella

The first thing I noticed was the smell.

My eyes opened and I was in a large tavern. It boomed with sound and reeked of alcohol mixed with musky colognes and sweet fruity perfumes.

My nose felt overstimulated, and I was forced to plug my nose with my hand in an attempt to nullify the stench, but I could still smell it.

I began to wonder where I was. I had never been in this bar before, so I knew I was not in a memory, not one of mine at least. Perhaps it was one of Odessa's and I was experiencing it through our empathy link.

I knew I was unconscious, that much was certain. I was just uncertain of why I was unconscious. There was no shortage of reasons, the shock of the water, the impact of the fall, general exhaustion.

I had hoped that I had been summoned by Eloah once more and perhaps he could have given me his Blessing once again, but he would not have fit in such a building.

Besides, this was no holy place. People danced merrily along to the beat produced by a group of bards that strummed ukuleles and beat on drums.

There were several couples slouched in ecstasy unable to keep their hands off of each other, their lips overlapping, and their eyes closed.

A man with a patchy beard and silver capped teeth reached his hand at a waitress's waist. She had pale blonde hair and dark green eyes that I could see shining from a distance and wore a short dress.

The waitress slapped him away with her hand and smiled at him as she chastised him with her finger going up and down.

"Come on, Arabella, no need to be dramatic. You can uncover your nose. The smell here is not that bad. You get used to it quickly," I heard her say.

I knew her voice. No one else sounded like her although her mother had spoken similarly. But it could not be possible. She had been killed by the First Constellation.

She was dead.

I looked away from the waitress and the man. I looked for the voice and across the table I sat at, I saw her.

Her dark grey eyes were studying me, waiting for my reaction. She looked like she had gained a bit of weight and under her eyes there were bags like she had not been sleeping well.

And she was smiling; all the more reason to believe this was a fabrication of my imagination. I had only seen Estella smile a handful of times throughout our lives together.

For it was Estella of Opulake seated across from me. I knew her for the white patch of hair above her forehead that contrasted with her head of black hair, but it looked like she had dyed the white patch and her hair was all black.

She even wore the purple stoned earrings I had gotten her, and they glittered in the light of the lamp that sat on the table between us.

In between us on the table was a rusty empty bucket and a plate of Estella's favorite dish which was roasted potatoes coated with cheese, but the plate remained untouched and looked cold.

"This is a dream," I said, not believing what I was experiencing.

"Yes, it is," Estella said smiling. "But that does not mean I am not real."

"This is a dream," I repeated. "Samson kicked me into the water. My body could not manage it so here we are."

Estella's smile faded.

"Samson? Samson is free? But he was captured by the Mystio," she said placing her hand on my shoulder.

"He got out," I said. "I went with the Mystio to capture him. What do you care? You are dead. If you were alive, you would not have left me at the mercy of the First Constellation."

Estella frowned like she did. She frowned with her eyes and when she did it seemed like storm clouds raced in a circle around her grey irises.

"Why would you do that?" she asked. "You are no fighter."

It was my turn to smile.

"I felt a calling; or rather I felt no calling. After you and Tripa Fons died along with Skylark and the rest of Opulake I was left alone. I am the last daughter of Opulake.

Estella placed her hand on mine, and it felt like the real one had. It was at that moment she saw my damaged hand and before she could ask about it, I answered her question.

My ring finger had been restored but the pinky finger was gone. I wondered if continued use of the Blessing would restore it over time or if it was gone for good.

"Hell hound," I said. "It hurt a lot, but it feels better now."

Estella's face was a combination of guilt and sadness. She was silent for several seconds before speaking again.

There were questions I wanted to ask Estella, but the Estella I knew would never have left me alone in Opulake. The woman I was speaking to was not her.

That woman had died my friend and this woman could not have been Estella of Opulake. Perhaps she was another doppelganger like I had fought on the tower.

She opened her mouth to speak but her face turned green, and her cheeks bulged suddenly. She reached for the bucket in the middle of the table and threw up quietly into it.

I looked away politely and waited for her to finish.

"You are not overdrinking again I hope," I said as she wiped her mouth.

"Nah," she replied. "I quit."

Estella had loved to drink even when we were younger. Her quitting was something I would never have thought the real Estella would do but before I could inquire about it further, she continued speaking.

"Come to South Dresden. You will find you are not the last daughter of Opulake as you believe," Estella said and her she finished she began to fade.

"If you are fighting Samson, Eloah give you strength. I can keep you here no longer. But do not die, Arabella of Opulake. Preserve yourself or else, *I* will become the last daughter of Opulake."

I looked into her storm grey eyes as a raindrop rolled down her cheek but before I could reply I was in the water.

My body temperature plummeted, and I immediately swallowed a mouthful of ocean water. I began to choke. It took a moment to orientate myself and I looked towards the green glow below me.

I flipped myself and began to swim towards the light hoping it was the cavern I had come from. My shoulder stung from the exertion and although I could swim, I was no Terra Barkley, who had swam across the Great River from South Dresden to North Dresden in protest of boat passage prices.

My lungs had water in them, and I could feel the exhaustion creeping into my limbs. I swallowed the water in my mouth, and it tasted of pure salt and against my will it seemed I tried to get more air but there was only more water.

Eloah.

I called for him but there was no answer. My vision began to blur but the surface was *so* close. I *had* to defeat Samson. Eloah had chosen me as his next prophet. There was no one else for the task.

I swallowed the water in my mouth once more and felt as if I would throw up, but I gulped hard and kept my lips sealed.

If I could have screamed I would have as I urged my body forward in a final push. My arms and legs felt as if they were on fire, yet at the same time they were freezing from the water. My chest burned and vision was blotted with blotches of blackness.

My fingers broke the surface and I attempted to use it to pull myself up, but I was not close enough to the submarine or the ground to grab onto them and it seemed an eternity passed before my face broke the surface.

I gave an almighty cough as I was able to breathe once more. I blinked several times and looked towards where the others had been.

A wall of large rocks blocked my view, and I could no longer see the First Constellation or any of the others.

I would have investigated the wall to see if I could have reached the others, but I heard a hum begin to emanate from the submarine and turned towards it.

Samson was there. Only I could stop him.

I said a quick prayer to Eloah and then began to swim towards the submarine. It was farther from the shore than it had been when we had departed it but as I arrived at the side of the submarine, I found a ladder on the side of it that I could grab onto.

I sighed in exhaustion and grabbed onto the ladder with one hand as the submarine began to pick up speed. Panicking I quickly latched onto the ladder with my other hand.

My legs were pulled from behind me by the water and I was dragged through the water with only my hands on the ladder. I grunted from the effort as I managed to pull my feet onto the bottom rung.

Just as I accomplished getting my body onto the ladder completely the submarine began to sink into the water, and I was forced to jump several rungs at once to reach the top where the submarine's entry hatch was.

It was locked tight and the process of turning it was slow going. Soon I would be submerged in the water and any hope of getting into the submarine without it flooding was fading fast.

I committed myself to opening the hatch and as the water climbed up my calves it swung open, and I jumped into the submarine.

I fell right into the arms of Samson. He caught me with a grunt and before I could react, he tightened his grip on me and threw me.

I screamed as I flew and cried out in pain as my back slammed into the metal wall of the submarine.

Water began to gush into the submarine, and I looked up in horror. It flowed downwards quickly and in seconds the water was up to my shins.

"The hatch!" I shouted.

Samson jumped upwards, easily grabbed the edge of the hatch, and pulled it closed. It seemed even he was not keen to fight the ocean itself.

He looked at me and sneered.

"Why won't you just let me leave? Your people are dead. Defeating me will not bring them back. I will be leaving the First Constellation. I will sail east, you will never see me again after today," he said.

It was probably the most coherent collection of sentences I had heard him ever speak that was not trash talk, but I was not swayed by his plea.

"I can not let you escape. You will face justice. Capturing you will not bring my people back, but I am not as alone as you think. I will not let you sail east; there are people I care about to the east. I would not unleash a murderer like you on anyone, especially not them. You are correct in saying I will never see you again after today, except mayhap in my nightmares. There is one thing you are wrong about, Lieutenant Samson."

"And what is that?" Samson said, his green eyes gleaming.

"I was sent as Eloah's Vengeance for your transgressions against his children. I am not here to capture you or defeat you. I am here to kill you."

Chapter TWENTY

tinosa

I was done talking.

I had fought Samson twice now and had not beaten him alone yet. This time would be different. It had to be. I had something more than Eloah's edict awaiting me after this adventure.

There was Estella in South Dresden. I had to believe it was her; it made me not feel so alone and gave me something to look forward to after this.

I was exhausted but I could see Samson was also tired. His chest rose and fell quickly, and he slouched with his arms hanging low.

Samson opened his mouth to speak but I did not care to hear what he had to say. I rushed forward and with my hands cloaked in my Faith I punched Samson quickly in the gut.

Samson doubled over and I felt something wet land on my neck. I cringed at the thought that it was blood or saliva, but I could not focus on it.

Leaving no time for Samson to recover when he lowered himself in pain, I brought my fist up and slammed it into Samson's chin sending him falling onto the submarine ground.

I wondered if someone needed to steer the vehicle as it continued unmanaged through the water. I would need to make this fight as quick as possible so I could get back to the others and Hong Tao.

I grabbed a heavy bag off a bench and after winding it in a circle I cloaked it in my Faith and slammed it into Samson's face.

His face went red, and blood began to flow from his nose. He spit a globule of blood and it landed at my feet surrounding one of his teeth.

Samson reached towards me with his hands wide and open. He took a single step but then the submarine crashed into something, and he was thrust towards me off balance.

I tried to land another blow while he was vulnerable but the force of the submarine shifting also sent me towards the back of the vessel.

Before I hit the ground, I felt Samson's hand grip my ankle. Before I could use my Faith somehow to free myself he tightened his grasp until I felt the bone crack.

I cried out in pain as the bone pierced my skin. I could see it protruding through the flesh and I felt myself getting faint.

"Ahhhhhhh!" I shouted as the nausea began to take over.

A small spout of water began to leak into the submarine from the ocean outside and the submarine creaked eerily. I had no idea how the leak had formed but I was grateful that it had taken Samson's attention off of me.

Samson glanced nervously back at the leak and in that moment, I pulled my foot out of his grip. It was a painful maneuver and even though I was free of his grasp my foot hung awkwardly.

I knew I could not put any weight on it. It would be impossible to fight as I had before. In fact, I did not know I could beat Samson at all with this injury, barring Eloah's intervention.

I glanced at Samson, worried now was the time that he would come and finish me, but he was more concerned with the leak in the submarine.

"We're too deep," he said, and I heard the submarine creak once more, shorter but louder. "We will be crushed soon. There is no point in fighting further."

He sounded defeated and he sat on the bench near the steering wheel and stared downward at his intertwined fingers.

My ears popped and I could sense something was off. I glanced uneasily from Samson to the hole in the submarine where the water was leaking in.

The hull of the submarine creaked, and it seemed its body was compressing slightly. I knew nothing of the submarine and the only one who might know what was going on was my enemy.

I wished once more that Odessa was here. She was from Pavrenes on the unnamed island, and I figured we were closer to her than Opulake now.

Odessa had spent her whole life there and I figured she knew just as much as I about submarines, but I could have used her words of encouragement.

Her father, Grimke, had trained her as a fighter since she was a child. Perhaps he had mentioned submarines in her studies.

I considered reaching out to her through our empathy link, but I knew she was focused on getting the plagicine to her father and that the journey was not going as simply as we had hoped.

She had the Mystio Adonis with her, who seemed very capable. After all, he was the same rank as Micah and Micah had defeated Samson easily.

I decided against it. I knew Odessa might have other obstacles for her to focus on. Using the empathy link did not use much magic but between my ankle and the submarine I would need every drop of magic I had left to make it out of this situation victorious.

Odessa was not here to save me. Eloah had not given me his Blessing again. I would have to figure this out myself.

Samson was ignoring me, and he had his eyes closed as he muttered something that I could not make out.

I focused on his words and recognized words of faith, although they weren't Elohan. Was he praying? Were those Shovi words of faith?

It seemed that after a life full of crimes that he had so joyfully committed, in the end Samson was scared. Scared of dying? Scared of judgement? Scared to face his victims?

I knew of the god Shovi. Although her presence was not as widespread as Eloah her religion was present in Damasyr but more so in Cypress.

"Shovi will not forgive you," I said to Samson. "She does not smile upon murderers or thieves or those who act selfishly. You will not go to the halls of

Penthesiliea or the fields of *Bonswa.* She will have a cage waiting for you in Dasani and you will freeze. Your fingers will fall off and so will your toes and you will spend a thousand years contemplating your transgressions and when Shovi is done with you she will hand you over to Eloah and he will toss you in the deepest pits of Masego alongside Sicily Blackhand and Hecate of the Branch and you will burn for the rest of eternity."

If Samson heard my words he did not respond. His fingers remained interlinked, his eyes remained closed, and his lips continued moving in prayer.

Kill him now.

"I can not," I replied to Eloah. "I can not move with my body like this."

My leg began to glow with the new golden light and I found myself missing my old neon green Faith. My hands also glowed and although my pinky did not return, my injured finger was healed.

I cried out as I felt the bone of my leg sink back into my flesh and when the glow faded all that was left was a scar about three inches long where the bone had pierced the skin.

Now kill him.

I stood up hesitantly and placed my weight on the leg but felt no pain. Eloah had completely healed my leg.

I was hoping he would have given me his Blessing once more, but he had not.

I took a single step towards Samson but suddenly the submarine creaked loudly and there was a metallic crinkling sound, and a wall of the submarine became distorted and jutted inwards sharply.

"What is happening?" I asked Samson and to my surprise he answered.

"The hole has compromised the hull. We would have died instantly if not for the magical wards protecting the *Tinosa*, but they are fading now and soon we will be crushed," he said.

His voice had lost the confidence and bass he usually projected when he jeered and bragged, and now he sounded sad and defeated.

It would be so easy to kill him right now. He would not have fought back. Eloah would have his vengeance. Opulake would have its vengeance. *I* would have my vengeance.

But I was not sure if I could kill him in cold blood while he prayed to his god, even if he had done the same to so many children of Eloah.

Besides, killing Samson would not save the submarine. For the moment I needed his help.

"How do we stop it?" I asked.

"We can not," Samson replied without looking at me. "We are too deep. We could sail higher, but we would not make it before the magical wards faded and we were crushed. It is hopeless."

"Would it be quicker to go up or back to Jormondor?"

"I am telling you there is no hope," he said but when I didn't reply he continued. "The surface would be closer."

"Can you steer the submarine?" I asked.

Samson was silent for a moment and then he nodded his head.

"You steer us upwards, and I will make sure we are not crushed," I said.

Samson hesitated so I yelled at him to hurry up with an authority I had not known I possessed, and he jumped up and rushed towards the front of the submarine.

I did not trust him. It was an uneasy alliance, but I had no knowledge on how the submarine worked and Samson had no magic as far as I knew. We would need to work together.

With that said, I was not sure how the pressure worked either. I did not know how to reinforce the wards either, but I began to focus hard on the issue.

The pressure increase was caused by our depth Samson had said. The problem was that the hole let the pressure in so with that logic we could fix the issue by plugging the hole.

I remembered when the submarine had crashed into something while we were fighting and figured that must have created the hole. Would sealing the hole fix the pressure issue?

I rushed over to the hole in the wall and placed my hand over it. I focused on my Faith and when I removed my hand the hole had been patched by a seal of my golden Faith.

"Okay, leak sealed," I said with a sigh. "Disaster averted."

I could feel the submarine rising and I wondered how much farther we had to go. I began to think on how I would handle Samson once we surfaced.

He did not want to die, that much was clear, so it was obvious that we would have to fight once more. I was Eloah's Prophet; I would not let Samson go. He had to die.

I considered going to the front to see if I could study Samson and see how he controlled the submarine. If I could catch him off guard that would give me a higher chance of success.

I silently crept towards the front of the submarine and glanced at Samson. Before I could learn anything, the submarine groaned, and another wall compressed, and the compression created another leak in the submarine's hull.

The second leak was followed by two more leaks. I rushed back towards the back of the submarine and studied the leaks.

I extended my arms, sighed, and then cast my Faith out over each of the holes and sealing the leaks. I sighed and listened for the sound of the submarines, wary that more leaks might appear.

The holes were relatively small, so it did not take much energy to seal them but creating so many constructs at once was strenuous.

"How close are we?" I asked Samson.

"Close!" I heard him call from the front of the submarine.

The submarine let out a hiss and a line of purple magic passed across the entire submarine and immediately the submarine walls began to close in, groaning, screeching, and creaking metallically.

"What just happened?" I asked.

"Magical wards are gone," Samson said and I looked at the submarine aware that I might have only seconds left of life.

The walls creaked inwards, and I groaned. I was still so tired. It was hard maintaining so many seals on the holes and I could feel the ocean pressing against my seals, looking for a weakness.

I thought of releasing the seals and reinforcing the entire hull of the submarine, but I did not know if a second of pressure could mean our death. After all, any magical protection we had from the wards was gone.

Once again, I cursed my own lack of skill. Better Elohan Morales would have no issue transitioning from individual seals to a larger construct.

But I was tired. I could not keep all the seals up at once, so I sighed, said a prayer to Eloah, and released the individual seals.

The walls of the submarine roared and grasped at me hungrily throwing my concentration off. I lifted my arms and attempted to cast a construct to reinforce the submarine, but I was so tired only golden sparks flew from my fingers as the magic failed to form the construct leaving me at the mercy of Eloah.

Chapter TWENTY-ONE

shovi

The submarine's walls raced towards me as if it were a sentient predator but then froze mid-contraction.

I glanced towards Samson, but the room had become so deformed I could not see him from where I was standing.

I rushed to a nearby window.

The glass in the window was cracked in a thousand fractured lines. I touched it with my finger, and it cracked once more before pieces of it fell onto the submarine floor. Looking through the hole the glass had left in the window I saw that we had surfaced.

Water continued to pour in through the submarine's puncture wounds and I knew even if we were safe from the pressure, it would not be long until the submarine would sink from water intake.

I did not know how I would reach the others now. The submarine was damaged beyond repair, and I had no *imperi.* Jormondor was lost to me, and the others would have to handle Hong Tao and Olympia without me.

Without the submarine and with the route to the ocean blocked by the wall of fallen rock I wondered how they would escape. Surely Lady Gorin knew of another way out, but would she help them?

The water was freezing, and I was beginning to lose sensation in my toes. I reluctantly stowed my thoughts of the others because my survival was paramount. I reminded myself once more that if I died, Talicia would lose her big sister and I exhaled deeply in preparation.

I rushed towards the hatch. As I reached for the ladder I heard Samson groan from the front of the submarine. I ignored him and glanced at the ladder to freedom. It was jammed in the up position, and I jumped towards it in vain trying to reach it and pull it downwards.

My body was sore and was only able to lift myself a few inches off of the ground. I knew Samson would be able to reach it, but I was unsure how I wanted handle him yet.

With just a little bit of magic I thought I could have pulled the ladder down with my Faith, but I had not an ounce of magic remaining. I might be able to squeeze it out, but the result could have been fatal, and I feared risking it.

I groaned in frustration. I was exhausted and bruised. I needed rest. But there was no time for rest. Water continued to pour in, and I could hear Samson stirring behind the wall of metal.

Eloah please do not forsake me.

There was no response but without waiting a moment longer I climbed onto the bench of the submarine.

I was also hoping to get out of the freezing water as I got on the bench, but it had already risen to the level of the bench so although my legs were safe the cold that had dug into my feet remained and my dress was drenched and icy.

I jumped towards the hatch, but the water made it difficult to jump and I was unable to get enough height and landed with a large splash on the submarine floor.

The water now reached my breasts, and my dress grew even wetter. With a huff I quickly climbed onto the bench once more.

I strode as far back as I could and then ran towards the bench's edge and sprung towards the ladder. I defied gravity and managed to wrap my right hand around the lowest rung of the ladder.

Gravity grasped me and I tightened my grip on the ladder and my weight pulled the ladder down with a jerk.

I was thrust into the freezing water once more, but I had managed to successfully free the ladder, so I did not focus on the cold that was creeping throughout my body.

I began to climb the ladder, but I heard Samson call out for me and froze.

"Woman!" he called and with a sigh I made my way towards the front of the submarine.

I saw Samson submerged in the water. He was angled in such a way that he was on his back. He had his chin up in an attempt to maintain his access to air, but he only had a minute or two before the water would flood his mouth and nostrils.

I saw that blood dripped from his wrist and saw that the submarine had contracted in a way that had pinned his wrist in between two pieces of metal.

The wrist bled because it looked like he had attempted several times to free himself and the metal had sliced the skin in response.

I had been ordered to kill him. I had *wanted* to kill him. But now, I did not feel as strongly even though he had killed so many Opulakis.

And his words of faith. Something about them made me more hesitant. He believed in something even if it was loosely. He was not the idiotic heathen I believed he was.

I had never killed anyone. I was not opposed to doing so in self-defense but this was far from self-defense.

Samson was trapped where he was. There was no need to fight him or kill him. Soon the submarine would sink, and the water would grasp him, and he would freeze or drown before Shovi took him for judgement.

And I was so exhausted. I was tired of fighting. I felt like I could have slept for a week straight.

Leaving him and letting the Mensae Ocean take him was different from killing him, right? It should have left my conscience clear, but it did not.

Why?

I considered saving him. For a moment.

I had no magic, and my body was bruised and battered. I would still need strength to make it to shore once I got out of the submarine and was not sure how far the swim would be.

Saving him was just not feasible.

I strode as quickly as I could towards him but with the water rising ever higher it was a slow journey. I got to where the metal walls almost touched and looked through the gap they left.

Samson locked eyes with me and there was nothing but fear in his emerald irises. He was helpless and it was possible that I could help me.

It did not matter that he had wronged me.

It did not matter that he had wronged Opulake.

It did not matter that he had wronged Eloah.

I thought of how I left the others behind in the tower of magic and how regretful I had felt when they had gotten hurt.

I could not live my life getting even and it was not in my nature to not help someone if I could.

Bracing my hands on each wall I grunted and pushed outwards. I needed space to get to him and after a moment of hesitation the walls retreated, and I rushed as quickly as I could to where Samson was.

I attempted to lift him higher first so that he could breathe longer but he groaned, "My foot, it's stuck," and I was forced to leave him be.

I gulped deeply and dove below the subzero water to inspect where Samson's foot was lodged. Like his hand his left foot was stuck in between another spot where the submarine had morphed.

I pulled at his foot until it cut his leg. A lazy drop of blood drifted up through the water and right past my face.

I gave up on moving the leg itself and focused on the metal around his leg instead. I wrapped my fingers around the bends of the metal and pulled at it, attempting to move it, but it remained in place.

I surfaced for air and gasped as my lungs burned.

"Your leg," I sputtered. "It is stuck."

"Cut it off," Samson said without hesitation.

The water was rising, and I could feel the cold spreading further throughout my body. We did not have much time, but I was reluctant to cut his leg if I did not have to.

"I have one more idea," I said and dove into the water once more.

I swam to where his leg was pinned and after a moment of struggle, I manifested my Faith weakly. It was harder to do so without breathing first and the water was so cold it was hard to focus on anything but hypothermia.

I cloaked my hands in my Faith thinly and gripped the metal once more and pulled at it. I felt it shift slightly and Samson was able to pull his foot higher, but it was still lodged in between the metal.

I groaned and urged the metal to part farther, but it ignored my persuasions. I continued to pull at it until I needed air once more.

"Cut it!" Samson urged once more as I surfaced, and I shivered. His lips were just barely above the water now.

I took a deep breath and dove under the water once more. The leg was stuck, and the metal would budge no further.

I shook my head in reluctance, but I saw no other alternative. I had to use what magic I could spare trying to move the metal and I knew Eloah would offer me no assistance in freeing Samson.

I tore my shirt so I could have it ready for a tourniquet to reduce the blood loss that I knew would be coming.

I steeled myself and manifested a sheet of aura as I had seen Savant do. I pushed the sheet forward as high as I could on Samson's leg, just above the metal.

I was hopeful that it would be a single slash, but the water slowed the speed of the construct, and my magic was weak.

The first slash dug deep into Samson's leg causing blood to leak out heavily. Samson's body thrashed in the water, and I urged him to be still with my hand.

Moaning I urged the construct further once more, but it was still not deep enough. With the thought that I only needed one more slash I gritted my teeth and severed Samson's leg just below his knee.

Blood mixed with the water around me, and the severed leg floated upwards to me. I grew lightheaded but forced myself to continue. I leaned forward and wrapped the strip of shirt around Samson's leg to reduce blood loss. After I was satisfied with its application I rose above the water.

I glanced at Samson before I focused on his pinned left hand and saw his head leaning sluggishly against the wall of the submarine.

"Thank you, woman," Samson said. He held up his bloody left hand to show that he had removed it, but it was a gory scene.

"My name is Arabella. Of Opulake as you well know," I said. "We need to do something about your hand first," I said but Samson shook his head.

"It can wait," he insisted and although I was not sure, I leaned under Samson's arm and allowed his weight to fall onto me.

I lifted him and took a deep breath before guiding us both towards the hatch of the submarine. I exhaled deeply and as the water rose, I used it to float upwards and reach the rim of the hatch.

I pulled us onto the top of the submarine and looked down. The water of the submarine was murky with blood. I had made sure to grab Odessa's scabbard and I had also found a bag that looked like Estella's.

What it was doing there, I had no idea. It had probably been stolen by Olympia too and I worried that she had her eye on Estella as well.

I wanted to see what was in the bag, but Samson groaned, drawing my attention. I looked at him and saw that although Samson had been freed, he was by no means safe.

We did not have much time before the submarine sank completely. He had still lost a lot of blood and I looked around and saw the shore about a hundred feet away.

I leaned forward and gritted my teeth in preparation. I began to tear the bottom of my shirt so that I could bandage his wrist injury, but Samson caught my wrist lightly.

"Do not bother," he groaned weakly.

I lifted my hands and looked at him helplessly.

"I will not live in a cage for the remainder of my life. With these wounds I will never fight again. I will go to the Halls of Dishonor where I can at least see my son once more."

The Halls of Dishonor were the halls of the Shovi religion for those who had strayed from the path but had once been one of her champions.

I thought about what that meant about Samson and although I did not think his son would be there, I did not speak on it.

"Thank you, Arabella of Opulake," Samson groaned and then he said no more.

I looked at his body not sure how to feel. I had wanted to kill him, yes. Eloah had decreed that I was to kill him. I had not done it on purpose, but now he was dead, and I had dealt the wound.

"Well done, my Prophet," Eloah said in my head, but I felt no pride at the triumph.

I glanced upwards and the sunlight was blinding after being in the darkness of Jormondor and I was forced to squint as I looked to the north where South Dresden lay and then to the south where Pavrenes was.

South Dresden was where Estella was and Pavrenes was where Odessa was. They were in opposite directions. I thought about both of my friends as I tried to decide where I was needed more.

Arabella and the Tower of Magic

Estella had quit drinking, which was a surprise
but also an improvement and although she had appeared
a bit under the weather it did not seem like she was in
any danger.

Olympia had been interested in Odessa. She had
taken the *imperi* and could be in Pavrenes already now. I
could not get back to the city of Jormondor and I could
only pray that the others were okay and that they had
defeated Hong Tao.

I reached out to Odessa through our empathy link,
but I got no response. I wondered if I had done the spell
wrong because it seemed whenever I tried I could not
reach her. It could also have been because I was so tired
and out of magic.

The submarine had not sunk into the ocean yet
and while it floated, I said prayers and meditated for a
moment, and I even said a prayer specifically for
Samson.

When I could not sit in the same place any longer
I pushed his body back into the submarine, and his body
went down with the submarine as it was swallowed by
the ocean.

With those bandits around no one would be safe
so as I arrived on the beach, I took time to light a fire and
warm myself. I ate two coconuts and slept deep into the
next day.

Once I rested I stood up and looked south. It would be a long journey but if Odessa was in trouble I would be there to help. Estella would have to wait.

Samson had been defeated and I had faith the Mystio would handle Hong Tao. That left only Olympia and Jesuit on my list.

I did not know if I would be able to kill them but as the Prophet of Eloah it was my responsibility to stop them from harming any other Children of Eloah.

Olympia had played me in the city of Jormondor but that would not continue any further. I would find her and stop her.

I was alone but there were still connections to live for. I would make sure Odessa was safe and then I would find Estella.

"I will not fail," I said aloud, and I remembered Eloah's words when I had asked him if my parents still lived and smiled.

"You are not alone."

End of Book Two

The World of Alphan II

Aid Towers: towers constructed during the reign of King Harlem that are spread throughout Damasyr and serve as an alert system across long distances; there once were eighteen but now only eleven remain

Alekisanit: the wielder of the sunfire sword *Sithos,* he was the first human to marry a dwarf

Alphan II: one of three planets that orbit the two stars Astria and Zaniah

Astria: the younger sun of Alphan II, it rises second and has a more orange hue

Banshees: different from spirits, banshees are the leftovers of powerful magic and have a deafening shriek and are seen as omens of death in Damasyr

Battle of Three Sides: a battle in Opulake between the citizens of Opulake, Laurens, Lord of Opulake, and the First Constellation

Battle of the Sojourners: the last battle between dwarves and humans during the Sojourner War, a tsunami during the battle eliminated most of the dwarves of Damasyr

Callyssia: a luck seer from Cypress, she possessed the wish sword, Kurama and was a great user of Djinni magic

Cypress: a jungle country to the southeast of Damasyr ruled by the Sea King

Damasyr: a kingdom formerly known as *Bruenor*, currently occupied by the second human kingdom

Deeds: Elohan acts done to be elevated within the Church of Eloah

Djinni: warlocks who bargain and serve as conduits spirits to gain elemental magical powers

Duskdelver Clan: the main guardian clan of the dwarves, they guarded kings, chiefs, and valuables

Dwarves: the race that ruled Damasyr when it was called *Bruenor*, although they are not much shorter than humans, they were given their name from the giants who lived in *Bruenor* before them

Eloah: the god of the Elohan Faith

Etsans: metal constructs spider/crab creatures that live in dwarven cities

Fairies: their existence is debated but they are believed to be pointed eared fey beings that usher the change of seasons in Damasyr

Giants: the race rose out of the ground two thousand years ago, although they did not name the land others called it *Gath*

Ghouls: revenants created to take a form of someone else, their bite and scratch can even turn the living into even stronger ghouls called Bonjou Ghouls

Green Lion Guild: a dark guild in Cypress that handles darker matters and are trained mercenaries

Hell Hounds: initially failed attempts to mimic the creation of true life, now used as tools for those who practice Shadow Magic and Blood Magic

Humans: the main population of Damasyr during the fourth era

Inamorata: a magic bond made between lovers, it is the ultimate form of intimacy on Alphan II

Imperi: a combination of metal and gemstone that allows one to move from one location to another

Ithil: the purple moon that orbits the planet Alphan

Jemny: the royal capital of Damasyr ruled by the Queen

Kurama: a sword with a pommel shaped like a fox spirit and a blade that shimmers with red light

Luck Seers: those who use dice to tell fortunes; those who use dragon bones are the most accurate

Mag Sticks: rods of magnesium used to easily create fires

Morale: a member of the Elohan faith who can Channel to a certain standard

Mystio: the first squad of the Damasyri military

Onryō: vengeful spirits that haunt those that wrong them; they have even been known to possess family members to accomplish their goals

Pigeons: used to deliver messages from settlement to settlement

Queenslen Forest: an allegedly haunted forest near Pavrenes on the unnamed island

Rangers: the third squad of the Damasyri military

Rebellion of New Crowns: in the year 1449 the previous dynasty was overthrown by Ragnar the Berserker and his descendants became the new rulers of Damasyr

Red Ember Spiders: spiders eaten for bursts of magic, they are among the most magical beings on Alphan II

Rutabaga Zaebos: the First Prophet of Eloah, founded the six holy cities

Sunfire: enchanted fire used to make weapons with unique features, the practice has become rare

Shovi: the god of the Shovi religion, more commonly worshipped in Umbar

Sithos: a sword held by the Forever Prince Alekisanit; it was able to burst aflame when the secret magic word was spoken

The Blessing of Eloah: a blessing from the god Eloah given to his chosen champion that serves as a boost of magic and physical prowess

The Eternal Flame: a green flame in the Opulaki Church of Eloah that was lit for over a thousand years before being extinguished

The First Constellation: the largest bandit group in Damasyr, they have remained active despite attempts from the Queen to destroy their organization

The Return: a prophecy concerning the return of the god Eloah to Damasyr

Tripa: a title given to a temple head leader in the Elohan Faith, they report only to the Queen and the Most Elevated One

Tyvent: a country of islands to the east ruled by a council

Umbar: a slaver country southwest of Damasyr, the people here are said to conduct magic sacrifices in pyramids made of white marble; they coat their weapons in a venom that prevents wounds inflicted by the weapons from being healed with magic

Vasenya Longsword: known as the greatest ranger of Damasyr before she was classified as a Dark Ranger, a former friend of Rutabaga Zaebos

Vetiti: forbidden actions for those who follow the edicts of the First Prophet Rutabaga Zaebos

Whey: a bread made with magic used to restore magic energy

Yandhi: a powerful fire manifestations created by dwarven fire magic

Zaniah: the elder sun of Alphan II, it rises first and has a more yellow hue

Z'etoile: a marshland country to the west of Damasyr full of sorcerers and ghouls

Glossary

achuka- uh-choo-kuh

addemire- add-duh-mie-er

adela- uh-del-luh

adonis- uh-don-is

aegea- uh-gee-uh

aiguo- ag-guow

alekisanit- aye-el-kih-san-it

allegra- uh-leg-gruh

almonaster- al-mon-nast-stur

almonastian- al-mon-nast-stee-en

alphan- al-fan

ambrocio- am-bro-cee-oh

analisa- an-nuh-lees-suh

arabella- air-ruh-bell-luh

arinia- a-ren-nee-uh

arkebay- ar-kee-bay

arugula- uh-roo-guh-luh

ase vertan- ah-say ver-tan

asia- ay-zhuh

astria- ass-stree-uh

augue- aw-gee

balthazar- bow-tha-zar

baluga- buh-loo-guh

barnabas- bar-nuh-bus

beidha- bead-duh

bentley- bent-lee

biawacheeitchish- bee-uh-wah-chee-itch-ish

bjorn- byorn

bonswa- bons-swuh

bruenor- broo-nor

callyssia- cuh-liss-see-uh

canis- cane-nis

chelsea- chel-see

chisam- ch-sam

cicero- sis-sir-ro

colden- coal-den

cypress- sie-press

damasyr- dam-muh-sear

damasyri- dam-muh-sear-ree

dedham- ded-ham

djinni- ji-nee

dresden- dres-den

drie- drie

drien- dree-en

eloah- ee-loe-uh

elohan- e-loe-un

elvira- el-veer-ruh

elyse- e-leese

estella- ee-stell-luh

estonia- ee-stone-nee-uh

eufaula- yu-fall-luh

fabiola- fab-bee-oh-luh

felicita- fuh-liss-sit-tuh

frigga- frig-guh

fulla- fool-luh

fussiladi- foos-sih-lawd-dee

harlem- har-lem

ichor- ick-chor

ichorian- ick-chor-ree-an

inamorata- in-nuh-mor-rat-tuh

imperi- em-peer-ree

isla- i-luh

ithil- ith-thil

jackdaw- jak-daw

jacob- jay-kuhb

jarl- jaarl

jemny- gem-nee

jemnan- gem-nen

jesuit- jess-su-it

joani- jown-nee

joel- jowl

jormondor- jor-mun-dor

judo- joo-doe

kurama- kuh-rah-muh

kuri- koo-ree

garcia- gar-see-uh

gath- gath

gianni- gee-on-nee

gorin- gor-ren

glorid- glor-rid

graham- gram

grimke- grim-key

hermes- er-mez

hong tao- hong-tow

hua- hoo-uh

laurens- lor-rens

ledonia- lee-doe-nee-uh

li- lee

lito- lee-to

lunaredi- loo-ner-red-dee

maia- mie-yuh

marva- mar-vuh

merica- mair-rik-kuh

micah- mie-cuh

minato- me-nuh-toe

mensae- men-sae

moesha- -moe-eesh-shuh

montoya- mon-toy-yuh

mudo- moo-doe

mystio- mist-see-oh

nani- non-nee

nori- nor-ree

numenor- noo-meh-nor

odessa- oh-dess-suh

opulake- opp-pew-lake

olympia- oh-limp-pee-uh

onryō- on-ree-oh

oqubay- oh-que-bay

padawan- pad-duh-won

pavrenes- pav-rens

pavreni- pav-ren-nee

pensilea- pen-si-lee-uh

penthesilea- pen-the-sil-lee-uh

pershing- per-sheeng

potiphar- pot-ti-fore

prern- prer-n

priyank- pree-yaank

queenslen- kweens-len

ramona- ruh-mone-uh

rutabaga- roo-tuh-bay-guh

resyr- ree-sear

reyna- ray-nuh

roshni- rosh-nee

roe- roe

salia- sail-lee-uh

samson- sam-sun

savant- suh-vant

scout- scowt

serrano- sir-rawn-noe

sithos- sit-those

sitka- sit-kuh

skylark- sky-lark

solace- soe-luss

sorbet- sore-bay

tachyon- tak-kee-yon

talicia- tuh-liss-see-uh

tamberli- tam-bur-lee

tawni- tah-nee

tanner- tan-ner

terza- ter-zuh

themyscira- them-mis-skere-ruh

tinosa- tuh-no-suh

tripa fons- trip-puh fons

tyvent- tie-vent

vasenya- vuh-sen-yuh

velma- vel-muh

verdant- ver-don-t

victoria- vic-tor-ree-uh

victorija- vic-tor-ree-uh

virginia- ver-gin-yuh

volo- voe-loe

whey- wae

ukiyo- u-kee-yoe

umbar- um-bar

umi- u-me

zaebos- zie-bose

zaniah- zuh-nie-uh

z-etoile- zeh- twowl

About The Author

Trilogy Davis is a writer with over 10 years of experience. He is also a painter and content creator.

YouTube: Trilogy Davis

Website: trilogyeffect.net

He has written *Odessa and First Constellation, Arabella and the Tower of Magic, When Life Gives You Pineapples,* and is working on book three in The Legends of Damasyr series.

Other than writing and content creation, Trilogy loves reading, gaming, and going to new places.